The Great Gatsby

The Tragic Tale of Wealth, Obsession & Lost Dreams in The Roaring Twenties

A Modern Translation
Adapted for the Contemporary Reader

F. Scott Fitzgerald

Translated by Tim Zengerink

Table of Contents

Preface
Message to the Reader

Rebuilding the Greatest Library in Human History

Thousands of years ago, the Library of Alexandria was the heart of global knowledge — a sanctuary where the wisdom of every known civilization was gathered and shared freely.

And then, it was lost.

Now, we're rebuilding it — and you are invited to join us.

At the Library of Alexandria, we've set out to make every book available to every person on Earth — not just in print, but in every language, every format, and for every reader.

Here's how we do it:

- **Deluxe Print Editions at True Printing Cost** - Order any book as a high-quality paperback, elegant hardcover, or stunning boxset — and only pay what it costs to print. No markups. No middlemen.
- **Unlimited Access to the Greatest Works** - Enjoy thousands of timeless classics — from Plato to Shakespeare to Tolstoy — in beautiful, modern eBook and audiobook editions. Read and listen without limits — for every reader, everywhere.
- **Modern Translations for Every Language & Dialect** - We're reimagining the classics in clear, accessible language — and translating them into every dialect imaginable. Everyone deserves to understand humanity's greatest ideas.

When you visit **LibraryofAlexandria.com**, you're not just accessing books — you're joining a global movement to restore, preserve, and share the wisdom of civilization.

Join us today at LibraryofAlexandria.com

Together, we'll ensure the light of human wisdom never fades again.

With gratitude,

The Modern Library of Alexandria Team

Visit:
www.libraryofalexandria.com
Or scan the code below:

Introduction

The Dream Behind the Curtain: America, Illusion, and the Death of Idealism

Few novels capture the paradox of the American Dream—its radiant allure and corrosive disillusionment—as powerfully as *The Great Gatsby*. Written by F. Scott Fitzgerald and published in 1925, this slim novel, once modestly received, has come to define not only the Jazz Age but the moral ambiguity and cultural unrest that still shape American consciousness. It is a story of beautiful illusions and broken dreams, of boundless hope and bitter endings. More than anything, it is the story of a man who built a fantasy so intoxicating that it became both his salvation and his doom.

In *The Great Gatsby*, Fitzgerald weaves a tale that at first glance glitters with glamour: dazzling parties, lavish mansions, and characters clad in silk and champagne. But beneath this polished surface lies a haunting meditation on love, loss, class, and the lies we tell ourselves in the pursuit of meaning. Jay Gatsby, with his mysterious past and obsessive pursuit of Daisy Buchanan, stands as a mythic figure—part romantic hero, part tragic fool. He is the self-made millionaire who has everything money can buy, except the one thing his heart desires. In this, he becomes a symbol of America itself—aching to fulfill a promise it never fully defined, and often failing to distinguish between dream and delusion.

Narrated by the quietly perceptive Nick Carraway, the novel unfolds not simply as a story of one man's rise and fall, but as a subtle, devastating commentary on a society intoxicated by appearances. Gatsby's world, centered around the fictitious communities of West Egg and East Egg, is populated by characters who are careless with their wealth, cynical in their love, and hollow in their convictions. Fitzgerald's brilliance lies in how he draws us into their glittering world only to show us its fragility. Beneath the jazz, the smiles, and the sparkling gowns lies emptiness—masked by excess and sustained by denial.

To understand *The Great Gatsby* is to confront a fundamental question: what happens when dreams—once noble, even pure—become corrupted by the very materialism they try to escape? What happens when the pursuit of happiness becomes an endless performance? In this introduction, we will explore the origins of Fitzgerald's vision, the historical context of the 1920s, the novel's complex characters and themes, and the enduring cultural impact that makes *The Great Gatsby* as relevant now as it was a century ago.

The Jazz Age and the American Mirage

F. Scott Fitzgerald was both a chronicler and a casualty of the Jazz Age. Born in 1896, he came of age during a period of great change—one marked by the aftermath of World War I, the rapid growth of industrial capitalism, and the wild euphoria of the 1920s. In that heady time, America was discovering new technologies, new freedoms, and new definitions of success. For many, the old rules of class and morality were being rewritten by bootleg fortunes, fast automobiles, and a youthful culture intoxicated by jazz, dance, and rebellion.

It was during this cultural explosion that Fitzgerald conceived of *The Great Gatsby*—not as a celebration of the era, but as a cautionary tale. He saw the emptiness behind the opulence. His vision was shaped by his own experiences: a romance with Zelda Sayre that depended on financial security, years of living beyond his means, and a deepening awareness that the wealth he had once craved did not fulfill his deeper emotional or artistic needs. In Gatsby, he created a character who embodies this contradiction—

someone who conquers poverty only to become enslaved by the illusion of what success should feel like.

The setting of the novel—Long Island's newly minted "Eggs"—captures the socioeconomic divide of the age. West Egg, where Gatsby resides, represents new money: flashy, self-made, and socially insecure. East Egg, home to Daisy and Tom Buchanan, embodies old money: inherited wealth, entitlement, and a rigid social code that resists outsiders. This contrast forms the backdrop for Gatsby's tragic pursuit: he is trying not just to win Daisy's love, but to penetrate a world that refuses to fully accept him, no matter how rich or charming he becomes.

The novel is filled with images of decay beneath the glitter. The Valley of Ashes, a bleak stretch of industrial waste between the Eggs and New York City, represents the spiritual and environmental cost of the American Dream. The eyes of Dr. T.J. Eckleburg—painted on a fading billboard—gaze over this wasteland like a forgotten god, watching silently as people chase pleasure and leave destruction in their wake. These images reinforce Fitzgerald's message: the dream of success, once rooted in freedom and self-determination, has been hollowed out by greed and spectacle.

Yet Fitzgerald doesn't condemn the dream itself. In fact, he admires Gatsby's capacity to dream, even as he mourns the tragic naiveté of that dream. Gatsby's flaw is not that he wants too much—but that he confuses the illusion of Daisy with the idea of true happiness. His dream, sincere yet misguided, becomes the mirror in which America sees itself—not as it is, but as it longs to be.

Characters and Symbols:
Obsession, Identity, and the Collapse of Meaning

Gatsby is often viewed as a romantic figure, and in many ways he is. He believes in love, reinvention, and the power of will to reshape the world. But his love for Daisy is built not on truth, but on fantasy. He wants not just the woman, but the past she represents—a moment of perfection frozen in time, untouched by reality. When he throws his extravagant parties, they are not for entertainment, but for hope—hope that Daisy will appear, like a goddess descending into his carefully curated world. That hope is his religion. And like many religions, it cannot survive reality.

Daisy Buchanan, for her part, is not the golden girl Gatsby remembers. She is beautiful, charming, and emotionally elusive—but also shallow, passive, and bound to the privileges of her class. She may feel fleeting affection for Gatsby, but she will not choose him. In the end, she retreats into the comfort of wealth, protected by Tom, whose brutality is excused by social position. Tom himself is the embodiment of patriarchal arrogance and racial superiority—a man who maintains control through force, tradition, and manipulation. In this triangle of Gatsby, Daisy, and Tom, Fitzgerald illustrates how love becomes a transaction, and how identity can be both constructed and crushed by social forces.

Nick Carraway, the narrator, is the moral compass of the novel—though even he is not without bias. A Yale graduate and veteran of World War I, Nick begins the story with the belief that he is tolerant, honest, and above the fray. But as he witnesses the unraveling of Gatsby's dream and the moral decay of the world around him, he is changed. His final judgment—that Gatsby is "worth the whole damn bunch put together"—is both an elegy for lost idealism and a rejection of the society that destroyed it.

Symbols abound in the novel. The green light at the end of Daisy's dock represents hope, desire, and the unreachable. The color green, often associated with money and rebirth, becomes a bitter irony—it promises fulfillment but delivers only longing. The eyes of Dr. Eckleburg symbolize the loss of spiritual direction in a materialistic age. Gatsby's parties, filled with strangers and empty revelry, stand as a monument to superficial connection and the erosion of authenticity.

Ultimately, *The Great Gatsby* is not just a story about wealth and romance. It is a story about the search for meaning in a world that has replaced substance with surface. It is about the tragic distance between who we are and who we pretend to be, between what we want and what we can truly hold. It is about the cost of believing in dreams that are not grounded in truth.

Legacy and Relevance:
Why Gatsby Still Speaks to Us

Nearly a century after its publication, *The Great Gatsby* remains one of the most studied, adapted, and beloved novels in American literature. Its influence can be seen not only in literature, but in film, fashion, music, and cultural criticism. It captures a moment in time, yet speaks beyond it. It reveals the seductive pull of aspiration, the destructive power of illusion, and the fragile beauty of human longing.

Fitzgerald's prose—lyrical, precise, and deeply poetic—continues to enchant readers. His ability to capture complex emotion in a single image or phrase makes the novel endlessly quotable and resonant. Lines like "So we beat on, boats against the current, borne back ceaselessly into the past" encapsulate the novel's core theme: the eternal struggle between forward hope and backward regret.

In our modern era, where social media creates curated identities and the line between appearance and reality grows increasingly blurred, Gatsby's story feels more relevant than ever.

We are still chasing green lights—still dreaming of perfect lives just beyond our grasp. We are still navigating a culture where wealth is mistaken for worth, and where success is often defined by how convincingly we perform it. Gatsby's tragedy is not just that he dies—but that his dream dies with him, and the world goes on, unchanged.

As you open the pages of *The Great Gatsby*, prepare to enter a world of shimmering surfaces and haunting depths. Prepare to be seduced and sobered. Prepare to meet a man who dreamed too hard, loved too blindly, and hoped too long—and who, in doing so, revealed something timeless about the human soul. Let this novel speak to your own dreams, your own illusions, and your own search for meaning. Because in the end, Gatsby's story is not just his. It is ours.

The Great Gatsby

Then wear the gold hat, if that will move her;
If you can bounce high, bounce for her too,
Till she cry "Lover, gold-hatted, high-bouncing lover,
I must have you!"

Thomas Parke D'invilliers

Part 1

In my younger and more vulnerable years, my father gave me some advice that I've been thinking about ever since.

"Whenever you feel like criticizing anyone," he told me, "just remember that all the people in this world haven't had the advantages that you've had."

He didn't say anything more, but we've always had an unusually open way of communicating despite being reserved, and I knew he meant much more than what he'd actually said. As a result, I tend to hold back on making judgments about people, a practice that has allowed many interesting personalities to open up to me but has also made me a target for quite a few tiresome people. Those with troubled minds quickly recognize this trait when they see it in someone normal, and that's how I ended up being wrongly labeled as a politician in college—simply because I knew the private sorrows of wild, unfamiliar men. Most of these confessions came without my asking for them. I've often pretended to be asleep, distracted, or coldly dismissive when I could tell by some clear signal that someone was about to share something deeply personal with me. The personal confessions of young men, or at least how they put them into words, are typically unoriginal and damaged by obvious omissions. Holding back judgment is a matter of endless hope. I'm still somewhat worried about missing something important if I forget that, as my father smugly pointed out, and as I smugly echo, a sense of basic moral standards is distributed unevenly from birth.

After bragging about how tolerant I am, I have to admit that my tolerance does have its limits. People's behavior might be built on solid ground or shaky foundations, but beyond a certain point, I don't really care what drives it. When I returned from the East last fall, I found myself wanting the world to be orderly and morally disciplined forever; I didn't want any more wild adventures that gave me intimate looks into people's souls. Only Gatsby, the man this book is named after, was different from my general reaction—Gatsby, who embodied everything I genuinely despise. If someone's personality is just a continuous string of impressive actions, then there was something magnificent about him, some intense awareness of what life could offer, as though he was connected to one of those complex instruments that can detect earthquakes from ten thousand miles away. This sensitivity wasn't the same as the weak suggestibility that people call the "creative temperament"—it was an incredible capacity for hope, a romantic eagerness that I've never encountered in anyone else and probably never will again. No—Gatsby ended up being fine in the end; it was the things that consumed Gatsby, the corrupt influences that trailed behind his dreams, that temporarily killed my interest in people's failed disappointments and brief moments of joy.

My family has been prominent and well-off in this Midwestern city for three generations. The Carraways are somewhat of a clan, and we have a family tradition claiming we're descended from the Dukes of Buccleuch, but the real founder of my family line was my grandfather's brother, who arrived here in 1851, paid someone else to fight in his place during the Civil War, and established the wholesale hardware business that my father continues to run today.

I never met this great-uncle, but people say I resemble him—particularly when compared to the somewhat stern portrait hanging in my father's office. I graduated from New Haven in 1915, exactly twenty-five years after my father, and shortly afterward I took part in that postponed Germanic exodus known as the Great War. I found the experience so exhilarating that I returned home feeling unsettled. Rather than feeling like the vibrant heart of the world, the Middle West now struck me as the frayed border of existence—so I made up my mind to head East and study the bond business. Everyone I knew worked in the bond business, so I figured it could accommodate one more bachelor. All my aunts and uncles discussed it as though they were selecting a preparatory school for me, and eventually declared, "Well—ye-es," wearing very serious, uncertain expressions. My father agreed to support me financially for a year, and after several postponements I traveled East in the spring of 1922, believing it would be permanent.

The sensible approach was to find an apartment in the city, but it was summertime, and I had recently left a place with expansive green spaces and welcoming trees, so when a colleague at work proposed that we rent a house together in a suburban town, it seemed like an excellent plan. He located the house, a worn cardboard bungalow for eighty dollars a month, but at the final moment the company transferred him to Washington, and I headed to the countryside by myself. I owned a dog—or rather I had him for several days before he escaped—along with an old

Dodge and a Finnish housekeeper, who made my bed and prepared breakfast while murmuring Finnish sayings to herself at the electric stove.

It felt lonely for about a day until one morning a man who had arrived more recently than I did stopped me on the road.

"How do you get to West Egg village?" he asked helplessly.

I told him. And as I continued walking, I no longer felt alone. I had become a guide, a pathfinder, an original settler. He had casually granted me the freedom of the neighborhood.

And so with the sunshine and the great bursts of leaves growing on the trees, just as things grow in fast movies, I had that familiar conviction that life was beginning over again with the summer.

There was so much to read, for one thing, and so much excellent health to be drawn from the fresh, life-giving air. I purchased a dozen books on banking and credit and investment securities, and they sat on my shelf in red and gold like freshly minted money, promising to reveal the brilliant secrets that only Midas and Morgan and Maecenas possessed. And I had the noble intention of reading many other books as well. I was quite literary in college—one year I wrote a series of very serious and straightforward editorials for the Yale News—and now I was going to bring all such pursuits back into my life and become once again that most restricted of all specialists, the "well-rounded man." This isn't merely a clever saying—life is much more successfully viewed from a single window, after all.

It was purely by chance that I ended up renting a house in one of the most peculiar communities in North America. The house sat on that narrow, vibrant island stretching directly east from New York—a place that boasts, among its other natural wonders, two remarkable land formations. About twenty miles from the city, a pair of massive egg-shaped areas, nearly identical in outline and divided only by a small bay, project into the most civilized stretch of salt water in the Western hemisphere—the vast, tame waters of Long Island Sound. These formations aren't perfectly oval—much like the egg from the Columbus tale, both are flattened where they meet the water—yet their physical similarity must constantly amaze the seagulls soaring above them. For those of us bound to the ground, what's far more fascinating is how completely different they are in every aspect except their shape and size.

I lived at West Egg, the less fashionable of the two areas, though calling it that barely captures the strange and somewhat ominous difference between them. My house sat at the very edge of the egg, just fifty yards from the Sound, sandwiched between two enormous estates that cost twelve to fifteen thousand dollars to rent for the season. The place to my right was massive by any measure—it was an exact copy of some French town hall in Normandy, complete with a tower on one side, brand new beneath a sparse covering of fresh ivy, plus a marble swimming pool and more than forty acres of lawn and gardens. That was Gatsby's mansion. Or rather, since I hadn't met Mr. Gatsby yet, it was a mansion where a gentleman by that name lived. My own house was ugly, but it was a small kind of ugly, and since it had been ignored by developers, I enjoyed a view of the water, a glimpse of my neighbor's lawn, and the comforting presence of millionaires nearby—all for eighty dollars a month.

Across the bay, the white mansions of upscale East Egg sparkled along the waterfront, and the story of that summer truly starts on the night I drove over to dine with Tom and Daisy Buchanan. Daisy was my second cousin once removed, and I had known Tom during our college years. Right after the war ended, I had stayed with them for two days in Chicago.

Her husband had many physical talents, and he had been one of the most powerful ends who ever played football at New Haven—he was a national figure in some ways, one of those men who achieve such intense but narrow excellence at twenty-one that everything that comes after feels like a disappointment. His family was extremely wealthy—even during college, the way he spent money freely was something people criticized—but now he had left Chicago and moved East in a way that was truly stunning: for example, he had brought a whole string of polo ponies down from Lake Forest. It was difficult to believe that someone from my own generation had enough money to do something like that.

I don't understand why they moved East. They had lived in France for a year without any real purpose, and then wandered restlessly from place to place, following wherever wealthy people gathered to play polo. Daisy told me over the phone that this was a permanent relocation, but I didn't believe her—while I couldn't see into Daisy's heart, I sensed that Tom would continue drifting endlessly, searching with a touch of longing for the intense excitement of some long-lost football game that could never be recaptured.

And so it happened that on a warm, breezy evening I drove over to East Egg to visit two old friends I barely knew. Their house was even more impressive than I had anticipated—a bright red-and-white Georgian Colonial mansion that looked out over the bay. The lawn began at the beach and stretched toward the front entrance for a quarter of a mile, flowing over sundials and brick pathways and vibrant gardens before finally reaching the house and climbing up its sides in brilliant vines, as if carried by the force of its own movement. The front of the house featured a row of French windows that now gleamed with reflected golden light and stood wide open to the warm, breezy afternoon, while Tom Buchanan, dressed in riding attire, stood with his feet spread apart on the front porch.

He had transformed since his days at New Haven. At thirty, he was now a robust man with straw-colored hair, possessing a somewhat harsh mouth and a condescending demeanor. Two gleaming, arrogant eyes dominated his features and created the

13

impression that he was perpetually leaning forward in an aggressive stance. Even the refined elegance of his riding attire couldn't conceal the immense strength of his physique—he appeared to completely fill those polished boots, stretching the upper laces to their limit, and you could observe powerful muscles rippling beneath his lightweight jacket whenever his shoulder shifted. His was a frame built for tremendous force—a merciless body.

His speaking voice was a rough, raspy tenor that reinforced the impression of irritability he projected. There was a hint of fatherly disdain in it, even when addressing people he was fond of—and there were men at New Haven who absolutely despised him.

"Now, don't assume my views on these issues are the last word," he appeared to be saying, "simply because I'm tougher and more masculine than you." We belonged to the same exclusive club, and though we were never close friends, I consistently felt that he respected me and hoped I would appreciate him, driven by his own rough, rebellious longing.

We chatted for a few minutes on the sunny porch.

"I have a nice place here," he said, his eyes darting around restlessly.

Grabbing my arm, he spun me around and gestured with his wide, flat hand across the entire view in front of us, which included a sunken Italian garden, half an acre of rich, fragrant roses, and a blunt-nosed motorboat bobbing against the tide just offshore.

"It belonged to Demaine, the oil man." He turned me around again, politely but abruptly. "We'll go inside."

We walked through a tall hallway into a bright, rose-colored room that seemed delicately connected to the house by French doors at both ends. The doors stood slightly open, their white frames gleaming against the fresh green lawn outside that appeared to extend partway into the house. A gentle wind moved through the space, carrying curtains inward at one end and outward at the other like pale banners, lifting them toward the ornate, frosted ceiling that resembled a wedding cake, before flowing across the wine-red carpet and creating shadows that rippled like wind across water.

The only completely motionless object in the room was a massive couch where two young women floated as if suspended on a tethered balloon. Both wore white, their dresses rippling and fluttering as though they had just drifted back inside after a brief flight around the house. I must have stood there for several moments, listening to the sharp crack and snap of the curtains and the creaking of a picture frame on the wall. Then came a loud thud as Tom Buchanan closed the back windows, the trapped breeze died away throughout the room, and the curtains, rugs, and the two young women slowly settled down to the floor.

The younger of the two women was someone I didn't know. She was lying stretched out completely at her end of the couch, perfectly still, with her chin tilted up slightly, as though she was carefully balancing something on it that might easily slip off. If she noticed me from the corner of her eye, she didn't show it at all—in fact, I almost found myself quietly apologizing for interrupting her by walking in.

The other girl, Daisy, tried to get up—she leaned forward a bit with a thoughtful look on her face—then she laughed, a silly, delightful little laugh, and I laughed as well and stepped into the room.

"I'm completely paralyzed with happiness."

She laughed once more, as though she had made an incredibly clever remark, and grasped my hand briefly while gazing up at me, assuring me that I was the person she most desired to see in the entire world. This was her particular manner. She whispered softly that the last name of the girl who was balancing was Baker. (I've been told that Daisy's soft whisper was simply meant to draw people closer to her; a pointless observation that didn't make it any less enchanting.)

At any rate, Miss Baker's lips trembled slightly, she gave me an almost invisible nod, and then quickly tilted her head back again—whatever she was balancing had clearly wobbled a bit and startled her. Once more, an apology nearly escaped my lips. Almost any display of complete independence draws an amazed admiration from me.

I turned to look at my cousin, who started questioning me in her quiet, captivating voice. It was the type of voice that draws your attention completely, as though every word she spoke was a unique melody that would never be heard again. Her expression was both melancholy and beautiful, filled with luminous features—sparkling eyes and a vivid, passionate mouth—but her voice carried an energy that men who had fallen for her couldn't easily dismiss: an irresistible pull, a soft "Pay attention," a hint that she had recently experienced wonderful, thrilling adventures and that more wonderful, thrilling moments were waiting just around the corner.

I told her about my brief stop in Chicago during my journey east, and how a dozen people had asked me to send their love to her.

"Do they miss me?" she cried with overwhelming joy.

"The entire town is empty and sorrowful. Every car has its left rear wheel painted black like a mourning wreath, and a continuous wailing sound echoes throughout the night along the northern shoreline."

"How beautiful! Let's go back, Tom. Tomorrow!" Then she added without any connection to what they'd been discussing: "You should see the baby."

"I'd like to."

"She's asleep. She's three years old. Haven't you ever seen her?"

"Never."

"Well, you should see her. She's—"

Tom Buchanan, who had been pacing restlessly around the room, came to a stop and placed his hand on my shoulder.

"What are you doing, Nick?"

"I'm a bond man."

"Who with?"

I told him.

"Never heard of them," he said with certainty.

This irritated me.

"You will," I replied curtly. "You will if you remain in the East."

"Oh, I'll stay in the East, don't you worry," he said, glancing at Daisy and then back at me, as if he were alert for something more. "I'd be a God damned fool to live anywhere else."

At this moment Miss Baker exclaimed "Absolutely!" so suddenly that I jumped—these were the first words she had spoken since I entered the room. Clearly it caught her off guard as much as it did me, because she yawned and then rose to her feet with a sequence of quick, graceful movements.

"I'm stiff," she complained, "I've been lying on that couch for as long as I can remember."

"Don't look at me," Daisy shot back, "I've been trying to get you to New York all afternoon."

"No, thanks," said Miss Baker to the four cocktails just brought in from the pantry. "I'm completely in training."

Her host stared at her in disbelief.

"You are!" He downed his drink as though it were just a drop left at the bottom of a glass. "How you manage to get anything accomplished is completely beyond me."

I glanced at Miss Baker, curious about what she had "accomplished." I found myself enjoying the sight of her. She was a slim, small-breasted young woman with perfect posture, which she emphasized by pulling her shoulders back like a military cadet. Her gray eyes, tired from the sun, met mine with courteous mutual interest from a pale, attractive, yet restless face. It struck me then that I had encountered her before, or perhaps seen a photograph of her somewhere.

"You live in West Egg," she said with disdain. "I know someone there."

"I don't know a single—"

"You must know Gatsby."

"Gatsby?" Daisy demanded. "What Gatsby?"

Before I could respond that he was my neighbor, dinner was announced; forcefully wedging his rigid arm under mine, Tom Buchanan steered me out of the room as if he were moving a chess piece to another square.

Gracefully and with relaxed movements, their hands resting gently on their hips, the two young women walked ahead of us onto a rose-colored porch that opened toward the sunset, where four candles flickered on the table in the gentle breeze.

"Why candles?" Daisy protested, her brow furrowing. She pinched them out with her fingertips. "In two weeks we'll have the longest day of the year." She gazed at all of us with a bright expression. "Do you always wait for the longest day of the year and then miss it? I always wait for the longest day of the year and then miss it."

"We should plan something," Miss Baker yawned, settling into her chair at the table as though she were climbing into bed.

"All right," said Daisy. "What should we plan?" She turned to me helplessly: "What do people plan?"

Before I could respond, her eyes locked onto her little finger with an expression of wonder.

"Look!" she complained; "I hurt it."

We all looked—the knuckle was black and blue.

"You did it, Tom," she said in an accusing tone. "I know you didn't intend to, but you definitely did it. That's what I get for marrying such a brutish man, a massive, hulking physical specimen of a—"

"I hate that word 'hulking,'" Tom protested irritably, "even when you're just joking."

"Hulking," Daisy insisted.

Sometimes she and Miss Baker spoke simultaneously, quietly and with a playful randomness that never quite became meaningless chatter, remaining as composed as their white dresses and their detached gazes in the complete absence of any longing. They were simply there, and they welcomed Tom and me, making only a courteous and pleasant attempt to entertain or be entertained. They understood that soon dinner would end and a bit later the evening would also conclude and be casually set aside. This was strikingly different from the West, where an evening was rushed from one stage to the next toward its conclusion, either in constantly frustrated expectation or in pure anxious fear of the moment itself.

"You make me feel uncivilized, Daisy," I admitted during my second glass of the corky but quite impressive red wine. "Can't you discuss farming or something like that?"

I didn't mean anything specific by this comment, but it was interpreted in a way I hadn't anticipated.

"Civilization is falling apart," Tom burst out angrily. "I've become incredibly pessimistic about everything. Have you read The Rise of the Coloured Empires by this guy Goddard?"

"Why, no," I replied, somewhat taken aback by his tone.

"Well, it's an excellent book, and everyone should read it. The concept is that if we don't pay attention, the white race will be— will be completely overwhelmed. It's all based on scientific material; it's been demonstrated."

"Tom's becoming quite deep," Daisy said, with a look of thoughtless melancholy. "He reads serious books filled with complex vocabulary. What was that word we—"

"Well, these books are all scientific," Tom insisted, glancing at her with impatience. "This guy has figured out the whole thing.

It's up to us, since we're the dominant race, to stay alert or these other races will take control of everything."

"We have to defeat them," Daisy whispered, winking intensely toward the blazing sun.

"You should live in California—" Miss Baker started to say, but Tom cut her off by shifting heavily in his chair.

"This idea is that we're Nordics. I am, and you are, and you are, and—" After the briefest pause, he included Daisy with a small nod, and she winked at me once more. "—And we've created everything that makes up civilization—you know, science and art, and all of that. Do you understand?"

There was something pitiful about how intensely he focused, as though his self-satisfaction, sharper than it used to be, no longer satisfied him. When the telephone rang inside almost right away and the butler stepped away from the porch, Daisy took advantage of the brief interruption and leaned toward me.

"I'll tell you a family secret," she whispered with excitement. "It's about the butler's nose. Do you want to hear about the butler's nose?"

"That's why I came over tonight."

"Well, he wasn't always a butler; he used to polish silver for some people in New York who owned a silver service set for two hundred people. He had to polish it from morning until night, until eventually it started to affect his nose—"

"Things went from bad to worse," suggested Miss Baker.

"Yes. Things went from bad to worse, until finally he had to give up his position."

For a moment, the last rays of sunlight touched her radiant face with romantic tenderness; her voice drew me forward breathlessly as I hung on every word—then the glow disappeared, each beam of light abandoning her with reluctant sorrow, like children reluctantly leaving a delightful street as evening falls.

The butler returned and whispered something quietly in Tom's ear, which made Tom scowl, shove his chair back, and walk inside without saying anything. As though his leaving had awakened something inside her, Daisy leaned forward once more, her voice bright and melodious.

"I love having you at my table, Nick. You remind me of a—of a rose, a perfect rose. Don't you think so?" She looked to Miss Baker for agreement: "A perfect rose?"

This wasn't true. I'm nothing like a rose, not even remotely. She was just improvising, but an exciting warmth radiated from her, as though her heart was attempting to reach out to you hidden within one of those breathless, captivating words. Then all at once she tossed her napkin onto the table and apologized before heading into the house.

Miss Baker and I shared a brief look that deliberately revealed nothing. I was just about to say something when she suddenly sat up straight and whispered "Sh!" in a cautionary tone. A muffled, intense conversation could be heard coming from the next room, and Miss Baker leaned forward without embarrassment, straining to listen. The voices wavered on the edge of being understandable, faded away, rose with excitement, and then stopped completely.

"This Mr. Gatsby you mentioned is my neighbor—" I started.

"Don't talk. I want to hear what happens."

"Is something happening?" I asked innocently.

"You mean to say you don't know?" said Miss Baker, genuinely surprised. "I thought everyone knew."

"I don't."

"Why—" she said hesitantly. "Tom's got some woman in New York."

"Got some woman?" I repeated, completely bewildered.

Miss Baker nodded.

"She could at least have the courtesy not to call him during dinner. Don't you think?"

Almost before I understood what she meant, there was the rustle of a dress and the sound of leather boots, and Tom and Daisy had returned to the table.

"There was nothing we could do about it!" Daisy exclaimed with forced cheerfulness.

She sat down, looked carefully at Miss Baker and then at me, and went on: "I stepped outside for a moment, and it's incredibly romantic out there. There's a bird on the lawn that I believe must be a nightingale that came over on the Cunard or White Star Line. He's singing his heart out—" Her voice became melodic: "It's romantic, isn't it, Tom?"

"Very romantic," he said, and then spoke to me with a dejected tone: "If there's enough light remaining after dinner, I'd like to take you down to see the stables."

The telephone rang inside with a jarring sound, and when Daisy shook her head firmly at Tom, the topic of the stables— indeed, all conversation—disappeared completely. From the scattered pieces of those final five minutes at the dinner table, I recall the candles being relit for no apparent reason, and I felt an urge to meet everyone's gaze directly while simultaneously wanting to avoid all eye contact. I had no idea what thoughts were running through Daisy and Tom's minds, but I suspect that even Miss Baker, who appeared to have developed a kind of resilient cynicism, couldn't entirely dismiss the piercing, mechanical insistence of this fifth presence from her thoughts. For someone with a particular disposition, the circumstances might have appeared fascinating—my immediate impulse was to call the police right away.

The horses, of course, weren't brought up again. Tom and Miss Baker, maintaining several feet of evening light between them, walked back into the library, as though they were keeping watch over a very real body, while I tried to appear politely engaged and somewhat hard of hearing as I followed Daisy through a series of connected verandas to the front porch. In the thick darkness there, we settled down next to each other on a wicker couch.

Daisy cupped her face in her hands as though she were feeling its beautiful contours, and her gaze slowly drifted out into the soft twilight. I could see that intense emotions were overwhelming her, so I decided to ask what I hoped would be some calming questions about her young daughter.

"We don't really know each other that well, Nick," she said suddenly. "Even though we're cousins. You didn't come to my wedding."

"I hadn't returned from the war."

"That's true." She paused. "Well, I've been through a really rough period, Nick, and I've become pretty cynical about everything."

Clearly she had good reason to feel that way. I waited, but she remained silent, and after a moment I weakly brought the conversation back to her daughter.

"I suppose she talks, and—eats, and everything."

"Oh, yes." She looked at me with a distant expression. "Listen, Nick; let me tell you what I said when she was born. Would you like to hear?"

"Very much."

"It'll show you how I've come to feel about—things. Well, she was less than an hour old and Tom was nowhere to be found. I woke up from the anesthesia feeling completely abandoned, and immediately asked the nurse whether it was a boy or a girl. She told me it was a girl, so I turned my head away and cried. 'All right,' I said, 'I'm glad it's a girl. And I hope she'll be a fool—that's the best thing a girl can be in this world, a beautiful little fool.'

"You see, I think everything's awful anyway," she continued with conviction. "Everyone thinks so—the most progressive people. And I know. I've been everywhere and seen everything and done everything." Her eyes darted around defiantly, much like

Tom's, and she laughed with exciting contempt. "Sophisticated—God, I'm sophisticated!"

The moment her voice stopped, no longer commanding my focus or convincing me, I sensed the fundamental dishonesty in her words. This realization made me uncomfortable, as if the entire evening had been some kind of scheme designed to manipulate my emotions. I waited, and predictably, within moments she glanced at me with a clear smirk across her beautiful face, as though she had just declared her place in some exclusive secret organization that she and Tom were part of.

Inside, the red room was filled with bright light. Tom and Miss Baker sat at opposite ends of the long sofa, and she was reading aloud to him from the Saturday Evening Post—her words flowing together in a gentle, monotone rhythm that created a calming melody. The lamp cast bright light on his boots and a softer glow on her autumn-yellow hair, while the light caught the paper as she turned each page with a graceful movement of her slender arms.

When we entered, she kept us quiet for a moment by raising her hand.

"To be continued," she said, throwing the magazine onto the table, "in our very next issue."

Her body made itself known through a restless movement of her knee, and she stood up.

"Ten o'clock," she said, seemingly reading the time from somewhere up on the ceiling. "Time for this good girl to head to bed."

"Jordan's going to play in the tournament tomorrow," Daisy explained, "over at Westchester."

"Oh—you're Jordan Baker."

I now understood why her face seemed familiar—that same appealing yet scornful expression had stared back at me from

24

countless newspaper photographs of the fashionable social scene at Asheville and Hot Springs and Palm Beach. I had also heard some tale about her, a harsh and disturbing story, but I had long since forgotten what it was.

"Good night," she said softly. "Wake me at eight, won't you."

"If you'll get up."

"I will. Good night, Mr. Carraway. See you soon."

"Of course you will," Daisy agreed. "Actually, I think I'll set up a marriage for you. Come visit frequently, Nick, and I'll somehow—oh—throw you two together. You know what I mean—accidentally trap you both in closets and send you out on the water in a boat, and things like that—"

"Good night," Miss Baker called out from the stairs. "I haven't heard a single word."

"She's a nice girl," Tom said after a moment. "They shouldn't let her run around the country like this."

"Who shouldn't?" Daisy asked coldly.

"Her family."

"Her family consists of just one aunt who's about a thousand years old. Besides, Nick's going to take care of her, aren't you, Nick? She's going to spend many weekends out here this summer. I think the home environment will be really good for her."

Daisy and Tom looked at each other for a moment in silence.

"Is she from New York?" I asked quickly.

"From Louisville. We spent our white girlhood together there. Our beautiful white—"

"Did you have a little heart-to-heart talk with Nick on the veranda?" Tom asked suddenly.

"Did I?" She looked at me. "I can't seem to recall, but I believe we discussed the Nordic race. Yes, I'm certain we did. It kind of snuck up on us and before we knew it—"

"Don't believe everything you hear, Nick," he advised me.

I casually mentioned that I hadn't heard anything whatsoever, and after a few minutes I stood up to head home. They walked me to the door and positioned themselves next to each other in a bright, welcoming rectangle of light. Just as I was starting my engine, Daisy urgently shouted: "Wait!

"I forgot to ask you something, and it's important. We heard you were engaged to a girl out West."

"That's right," Tom confirmed warmly. "We heard that you were engaged."

"It's a lie. I'm too poor."

"But we heard it," Daisy insisted, catching me off guard as she opened up again like a blooming flower. "We heard it from three people, so it has to be true."

Of course I understood what they were talking about, but I wasn't interested in the slightest. The fact that gossip had announced our engagement was one of the reasons I had moved East. You can't stop seeing an old friend because of rumors, and at the same time I had no plans to be pushed into marriage by gossip.

Their interest actually moved me and made them seem less distantly wealthy—still, I felt confused and somewhat disgusted as I drove away. It seemed to me that Daisy should have rushed out of the house with her child in her arms—but clearly she had no such plans. As for Tom, the fact that he "had some woman in New York" was actually less shocking than discovering that a book had left him feeling depressed. Something was causing him to toy with worn-out ideas as though his robust physical self-centeredness could no longer satisfy his demanding heart.

Already it was deep summer on roadhouse roofs and in front of roadside gas stations, where new red gas pumps sat in pools of light, and when I reached my property at West Egg I drove the car under its garage and sat for a while on an old grass roller in the yard. The wind had died down, leaving a loud, bright night, with wings flapping in the trees and a constant organ-like sound as the full breath of the earth filled the frogs with life. The outline of a moving cat shifted across the moonlight, and, turning my head to watch it, I saw that I wasn't alone—fifty feet away a figure had stepped out from the shadow of my neighbor's mansion and was standing with his hands in his pockets looking at the silver specks of the stars. Something in his relaxed movements and the confident way his feet were planted on the lawn suggested that it was Mr. Gatsby himself, who had come out to figure out what portion of our local sky belonged to him.

I decided to call out to him. Miss Baker had brought him up during dinner, and that would serve as a good enough introduction. However, I didn't call to him because he suddenly gave me the impression that he preferred to be by himself—he extended his arms toward the dark water in an odd manner, and even though I was quite far from him, I could have sworn he was shaking. Without thinking, I looked toward the sea—and saw nothing except a single green light, tiny and distant, that could have been at the end of a pier. When I searched for Gatsby again, he had disappeared, and I found myself alone once more in the restless darkness.

———————

Part 2

About halfway between West Egg and New York, the highway quickly merges with the railroad tracks and runs alongside them for a quarter mile, as if trying to avoid a particular barren stretch of land. This place is a valley of ashes—an extraordinary wasteland where ashes pile up like wheat into mounds and hills and bizarre gardens; where ashes form the shapes of houses and smokestacks and rising smoke and, ultimately, through some remarkable transformation, ash-gray men who move faintly and seem to be disintegrating as they drift through the dusty air. Every so often, a train of gray cars creeps along an unseen track, lets out an eerie groan, and stops, and right away the ash-gray men emerge with heavy shovels and create a thick cloud of dust that hides whatever mysterious work they're doing from view.

But above the gray landscape and the bursts of desolate dust that drift continuously across it, you notice, after a moment, the eyes of Doctor T. J. Eckleburg. Doctor T. J. Eckleburg's eyes are blue and enormous—their retinas stand one yard tall. They stare out from no face, but rather from a pair of massive yellow glasses that hover over a nose that doesn't exist. Apparently some eccentric eye doctor placed them there to boost his business in Queens, and then either descended into permanent blindness himself, or simply forgot about them and relocated. But those eyes, faded somewhat by countless days without fresh paint, exposed to sun and rain, continue to watch over the somber wasteland.

The valley of ashes is bordered on one side by a small, polluted river, and when the drawbridge is raised to allow barges to pass through, passengers on the waiting trains can gaze at the bleak landscape for up to half an hour. There's always a stop there lasting at least a minute, and it was during one of these stops that I first encountered Tom Buchanan's mistress.

The fact that he had one was something people insisted on wherever he was known. His friends resented how he would show up at popular cafés with her and, after leaving her at a table, would wander around chatting with anyone he recognized. Although I was curious to see her, I had no interest in actually meeting her— but I did. I traveled up to New York with Tom on the train one afternoon, and when we stopped by the ash-heaps he jumped up and, grabbing my elbow, practically dragged me off the train.

"We're getting off," he insisted. "I want you to meet my girl."

I think he had drunk quite a bit at lunch, and his insistence on having me join him was almost aggressive. He arrogantly assumed that I had nothing better to do on a Sunday afternoon.

I followed him over a low whitewashed railroad fence, and we walked back a hundred yards along the road under Doctor Eckleburg's unwavering gaze. The only building visible was a small block of yellow brick positioned at the edge of the wasteland, functioning like a miniature Main Street serving the area, yet connected to absolutely nothing. One of the three shops housed within was available for rent and another was an all-night restaurant, reached by a path of ashes; the third was a garage— Repairs. George B. Wilson. Cars bought and sold.—and I followed Tom inside.

The inside looked run-down and empty; the only vehicle in sight was a dust-covered wreck of a Ford that sat hunched in a dark corner. I had started to think that this sorry excuse for a garage must be a front, and that luxurious and exotic living quarters were hidden upstairs, when the owner himself emerged from an office doorway, cleaning his hands with a rag. He was a fair-haired, lifeless man, pale, and somewhat good-looking. When he spotted us, a wet glimmer of hope flickered in his pale blue eyes.

"Hello, Wilson, old friend," said Tom, giving him a friendly slap on the shoulder. "How's business going?"

"I can't complain," Wilson replied, though his tone suggested otherwise. "When are you going to sell me that car?"

"Next week; I've got my guy working on it right now."

"He works pretty slowly, doesn't he?"

"No, he doesn't," Tom said coldly. "And if that's how you feel about it, maybe I should sell it somewhere else after all."

"I don't mean that," Wilson explained quickly. "I just meant—"

His voice trailed off and Tom looked around the garage with obvious impatience. Then I heard footsteps on the stairs, and within moments a woman's stocky silhouette appeared in the office doorway, blocking the light. She was somewhere in her mid-thirties and somewhat heavy, but she moved with the kind of sensual grace that some women possess naturally. Her face, framed above a spotted dark blue crepe dress, held no hint of conventional beauty, but she radiated an unmistakable energy, as though every nerve in her body was constantly alive and burning. She smiled deliberately and, walking past her husband as though he didn't exist, extended her hand to Tom while looking directly into his eyes. Then she moistened her lips and, without bothering to turn around, addressed her husband in a voice that was both gentle and rough:

"Get some chairs, why don't you, so somebody can sit down."

"Oh, absolutely," Wilson quickly agreed, and headed toward the small office, blending instantly with the cement-colored walls. A white, ash-like dust covered his dark suit and light hair just as it covered everything nearby—everything except his wife, who stepped closer to Tom.

"I want to see you," Tom said with intensity. "Catch the next train."

"All right."

"I'll meet you by the newsstand on the lower level."

She nodded and stepped back from him just as George Wilson came out of his office carrying two chairs.

We waited for her further down the road where we couldn't be seen. It was several days before the Fourth of July, and a thin, pale Italian child was placing firecrackers in a line along the railroad tracks.

"Terrible place, isn't it," said Tom, exchanging a frown with Doctor Eckleburg.

"Awful."

"It does her good to get away."

"Doesn't her husband object?"

"Wilson? He thinks she goes to see her sister in New York. He's so stupid he doesn't even realize he's breathing."

So Tom Buchanan and his girlfriend and I traveled up to New York together—or not exactly together, since Mrs. Wilson sat tactfully in a different car. Tom showed that much consideration for the feelings of those East Egg residents who might be on the train.

She had changed into a brown patterned muslin dress that pulled tightly across her somewhat broad hips as Tom assisted her onto the platform in New York. She purchased a copy of Town Tattle and a movie magazine at the newsstand, then stopped at the station pharmacy to buy some cold cream and a small bottle of perfume. Upstairs, in the grand echoing concourse, she allowed four taxis to pass by before choosing a fresh one—lavender-colored with gray interior—and we glided away from the crowded station into the bright sunlight. However, she immediately turned away from the window and leaned forward to tap on the glass partition.

"I want to get one of those dogs," she said with genuine enthusiasm. "I want to get one for the apartment. They're wonderful to have around—a dog."

We backed up to an elderly gray-haired man who looked remarkably similar to John D. Rockefeller. In a basket hanging from his neck huddled a dozen newborn puppies of mixed breeding.

"What kind are they?" Mrs. Wilson asked eagerly as he approached the taxi window.

"All kinds. What kind do you want, lady?"

"I'd like to get one of those police dogs; I don't suppose you have that kind?"

The man looked uncertainly into the basket, thrust his hand inside and pulled one out, squirming, by the back of the neck.

"That's no police dog," said Tom.

"No, it's not exactly a police dog," the man said, his voice tinged with disappointment. "It's more like an Airedale." He ran his hand across the brown, washrag-textured back. "Look at that coat. What a coat. That's a dog that will never give you trouble by catching cold."

"I think it's adorable," Mrs. Wilson said with enthusiasm. "What's the price?"

"That dog?" He gazed at it with admiration. "That dog will cost you ten dollars."

The Airedale—there was definitely an Airedale mixed in somewhere, even though its paws were surprisingly white—was passed over and made itself comfortable in Mrs. Wilson's lap, where she lovingly stroked its weather-resistant fur with delight.

"Is it a boy or a girl?" she asked gently.

"That dog? That dog's a boy."

"It's a female dog," said Tom decisively. "Here's your money. Go and buy ten more dogs with it."

We drove over to Fifth Avenue on that warm, gentle summer Sunday afternoon, the atmosphere so peaceful it felt almost like the countryside. I wouldn't have been surprised to see a large flock of white sheep rounding the corner.

"Wait," I said, "I have to leave you here."

"No you don't," Tom interrupted quickly. "Myrtle will be hurt if you don't come up to the apartment. Won't you, Myrtle?"

"Come on," she insisted. "I'll call my sister Catherine. People who should know say she's very beautiful."

"Well, I'd like to, but—"

We continued on, turning back across the Park toward the West Hundreds. At 158th Street the taxi came to a stop at one section of a long white row of apartment buildings. Casting a majestic, triumphant look around the neighborhood, Mrs. Wilson collected her dog and her other purchases, and walked proudly inside.

"I'm going to have the McKees come up," she announced as we rode up in the elevator. "And, of course, I need to call my sister, too."

The apartment occupied the top floor—a compact living room, a compact dining room, a compact bedroom, and a bathroom. The living room was packed to the doorways with a collection of tapestried furniture far too large for the space, making it impossible to walk around without constantly tripping over scenes of ladies swinging in the gardens of Versailles. The sole picture was an oversized photograph that appeared to show a hen perched on a blurry rock. When viewed from across the room, though, the hen transformed into a bonnet, and the face of a heavy-set elderly woman smiled down into the space. Several old issues of Town Tattle were scattered on the table alongside a copy of Simon Called Peter and some of the small scandal magazines from Broadway. Mrs. Wilson's first priority was the dog. An unwilling elevator boy fetched a box filled with straw and some milk, adding on his own a tin of large, hard dog biscuits—one of which slowly dissolved without enthusiasm in the milk saucer throughout the afternoon. In the meantime, Tom retrieved a bottle of whisky from a locked bureau drawer.

I have only been drunk twice in my entire life, and that afternoon was the second time; so everything that occurred has a foggy, unclear quality to it, even though the apartment was filled with bright sunlight until well past eight o'clock. While sitting on Tom's lap, Mrs. Wilson made several phone calls; then we ran out of cigarettes, and I went out to purchase some at the drugstore on the corner. When I returned, both of them had vanished, so I sat down quietly in the living room and read a chapter of Simon Called Peter—either it was awful writing or the whisky was affecting my perception, because none of it made any sense to me.

Just as Tom and Myrtle returned (after our first drink, Mrs. Wilson and I had started using each other's first names), guests began showing up at the apartment door.

Catherine, the sister, was a thin, sophisticated woman around thirty years old, with a thick, sleek bob of red hair and skin dusted with milky white powder. She had plucked her eyebrows and redrawn them at a more daring angle, but nature's attempt to restore their original shape gave her face a smudged appearance. Whenever she moved, there was a constant clicking sound as countless ceramic bracelets jangled back and forth on her arms. She entered with such an authoritative rush and gazed around at the furniture so possessively that I wondered whether she actually lived there. However, when I asked her about it, she laughed excessively, repeated my question out loud, and informed me that she lived with a female friend at a hotel.

Mr. McKee was a pale, delicate man who lived in the apartment downstairs. He had recently shaved, as evidenced by a white dab of shaving cream still clinging to his cheekbone, and he greeted everyone in the room with utmost politeness. He told me he worked in the "artistic field," and I later learned he was a photographer who had created the faded enlargement of Mrs. Wilson's mother that hung ghostlike on the wall. His wife was sharp-voiced, listless, attractive, and awful. She proudly informed me that her husband had taken her photograph one hundred and twenty-seven times since their wedding.

Mrs. Wilson had changed her outfit some time earlier and was now dressed in an elaborate afternoon gown made of cream-colored chiffon that rustled continuously as she moved around the room. Along with the influence of the dress, her personality had also transformed. The intense energy that had been so striking in the garage was now converted into impressive arrogance. Her laughter, her gestures, and her statements became more dramatically artificial with each passing moment, and as she expanded her presence, the room seemed to shrink around her, until she appeared to be spinning on a loud, creaking axis through the smoky air.

"My dear," she called out to her sister in a shrill, affected voice, "most of these guys will rip you off every single time. All they care about is money. I had a woman come up here last week to examine my feet, and when she handed me the bill you would have thought she had performed surgery to remove my appendix."

"What was the woman's name?" asked Mrs. McKee.

"Mrs. Eberhardt. She goes around looking at people's feet in their own homes."

"I like your dress," remarked Mrs. McKee, "I think it's adorable."

Mrs. Wilson dismissed the compliment by raising her eyebrow with contempt.

"It's just some crazy old thing," she said. "I just throw it on sometimes when I don't care how I look."

"But it looks wonderful on you, if you know what I mean," Mrs. McKee continued. "If Chester could just capture you in that pose, I think he could really make something special out of it."

We all stared silently at Mrs. Wilson, who brushed a strand of hair away from her eyes and smiled back at us brilliantly. Mr. McKee studied her carefully with his head tilted to one side, then slowly moved his hand back and forth in front of his face.

"I should adjust the lighting," he said after a moment. "I want to emphasize the contours of the facial features. And I'd try to capture all of the hair at the back."

"I wouldn't think of changing the light," cried Mrs. McKee. "I think it's—"

Her husband said "Sh!" and we all turned our attention back to the topic, at which point Tom Buchanan let out an audible yawn and stood up.

"You McKees should have something to drink," he said. "Get some more ice and mineral water, Myrtle, before everyone falls asleep."

"I told that boy about the ice." Myrtle lifted her eyebrows in frustration at the unreliability of the working class. "These people! You have to constantly stay on top of them."

She looked at me and laughed for no reason. Then she bounced over to the dog, kissed it passionately, and rushed into the kitchen, acting as if a dozen chefs were waiting there for her instructions.

"I've done some nice things out on Long Island," declared Mr. McKee.

Tom stared at him with a blank expression.

"We have two of them framed and hanging downstairs."

"Two what?" Tom demanded.

"Two studies. One of them I call Montauk Point—The Gulls, and the other I call Montauk Point—The Sea."

The sister Catherine sat down next to me on the couch.

"Do you live down on Long Island, too?" she asked.

"I live at West Egg."

"Really? I was at a party there about a month ago. At a man named Gatsby's place. Do you know him?"

"I live next door to him."

"Well, people say he's either a nephew or a cousin of Kaiser Wilhelm. That's where all his wealth comes from."

"Really?"

She nodded.

"I'm afraid of him. I wouldn't want him to have any dirt on me."

This fascinating information about my neighbor was interrupted when Mrs. McKee suddenly pointed at Catherine:

"Chester, I think you could do something with her," she suddenly said, but Mr. McKee just nodded in a disinterested way and shifted his attention to Tom.

"I'd like to do more work on Long Island, if I could get the opportunity. All I ask is that they give me a chance to begin."

"Ask Myrtle," Tom said, bursting into a brief laugh as Mrs. Wilson walked in carrying a tray. "She'll write you a letter of introduction, won't you, Myrtle?"

"Do what?" she asked, startled.

"You'll give McKee a letter of introduction to your husband, so he can do some studies of him." His lips moved silently for a moment as he came up with the idea, " 'George B. Wilson at the Gas Station,' or something along those lines."

Catherine leaned in close to me and whispered in my ear:

"Neither of them can stand the person they're married to."

"Can't they?"

"I can't stand them." She glanced at Myrtle and then at Tom. "What I'm saying is, why keep living with them if they can't stand them? If I were in their position, I'd get a divorce and marry each other immediately."

"Doesn't she like Wilson either?"

The response to this was surprising. It came from Myrtle, who had caught the question, and it was aggressive and vulgar.

"You see," Catherine exclaimed triumphantly. She dropped her voice again. "It's actually his wife who's keeping them separated. She's Catholic, and they don't believe in divorce."

Daisy wasn't Catholic, and I was somewhat surprised by how elaborate the lie was.

"When they do get married," Catherine went on, "they're heading out West to live for a while until things settle down."

"It would be more discreet to go to Europe."

"Oh, do you like Europe?" she exclaimed with surprise. "I just returned from Monte Carlo."

"Really."

"Just last year, I went over there with another girl."

"Are you staying long?"

"No, we just went to Monte Carlo and back. We traveled through Marseilles. We had over twelve hundred dollars when we started, but we got cheated out of all of it in two days in the private gambling rooms. We had a terrible time getting back, I can tell you. God, how I hated that town!"

The late afternoon sky appeared in the window for a moment like the blue honey of the Mediterranean—then Mrs. McKee's sharp voice brought me back into the room.

"I almost made a terrible mistake myself," she said with conviction. "I nearly married a Jewish man who had been pursuing me for years. I knew he wasn't good enough for me. Everyone kept telling me: 'Lucille, that man is completely beneath you!' But if I hadn't met Chester, he definitely would have won me over."

"Yes, but listen," said Myrtle Wilson, nodding her head up and down, "at least you didn't marry him."

"I know I didn't."

"Well, I married him," said Myrtle, ambiguously. "And that's the difference between your case and mine."

"Why did you, Myrtle?" Catherine demanded. "Nobody forced you to."

Myrtle thought it over.

"I married him because I thought he was a gentleman," she said at last. "I believed he understood what it meant to have class, but he wasn't worthy enough to clean my shoes."

"You were crazy about him for a while," said Catherine.

"Crazy about him!" Myrtle exclaimed in disbelief. "Who told you I was crazy about him? I was never any more infatuated with him than I was with that man over there."

She suddenly pointed at me, and everyone turned to look at me with accusation in their eyes. I tried to show through my expression that I didn't expect any kindness from them.

"The only time I was crazy was when I married him. I realized immediately that I had made a mistake. He had borrowed someone's best suit for the wedding and never even mentioned it to me, and the owner showed up one day while he was gone: 'Oh, is that your suit?' I asked. 'This is the first I've ever heard about it.' But I handed it over to him and then I went to bed and cried my heart out all afternoon."

"She really should get away from him," Catherine continued, speaking to me. "They've been living above that garage for eleven years. And Tom's the first boyfriend she's ever had."

The second bottle of whisky was now being constantly passed around by everyone there, except for Catherine, who "felt just as good on nothing at all." Tom called for the janitor and had him bring some famous sandwiches that were filling enough to serve as a complete dinner by themselves. I wanted to leave and walk east toward the park through the gentle twilight, but every time I attempted to go, I got caught up in some intense, loud argument that dragged me back into my chair as if I were tied down with ropes. Still, high above the city, our row of lit yellow windows must have added to the human mysteries that any random observer on the darkening streets below might notice, and I could picture him too, gazing upward and wondering what was happening inside. I found myself both inside and outside the scene at once, simultaneously captivated and disgusted by life's endless complexity.

Myrtle moved her chair next to mine, and all at once her warm breath washed over me as she told the story of how she first met Tom.

"It was on those two little seats facing each other that are always the last ones left on the train. I was heading up to New York to visit my sister and stay the night. He wore a formal suit and shiny patent leather shoes, and I couldn't stop staring at him, but whenever he glanced my way I had to pretend I was looking at the advertisement above his head. When we pulled into the station he was right beside me, and his crisp white shirt front pressed against my arm, so I told him I'd have to call a policeman, but he knew I was lying. I was so thrilled that when I climbed into a taxi with him I barely realized I wasn't stepping onto a subway train. All I could think about, again and again, was 'You can't live forever; you can't live forever.'"

She turned to Mrs. McKee and the room filled with her fake laughter.

"My dear," she exclaimed, "I'm going to give you this dress once I'm finished with it. I need to buy another one tomorrow. I'm going to write down everything I need to get. A massage and a hair wave, and a collar for the dog, and one of those adorable little ashtrays where you press a spring, and a wreath with a black silk bow for mother's grave that will last the entire summer. I have to make a list so I don't forget all the things I need to do."

It was nine o'clock—almost right after that I checked my watch and discovered it was ten. Mr. McKee had fallen asleep in a chair with his hands balled into fists resting on his lap, resembling a portrait of someone ready for action. I pulled out my handkerchief and cleaned the dried shaving cream from his cheek that had been bothering me all afternoon.

The small dog sat on the table, staring with sightless eyes through the haze of smoke, occasionally letting out weak whimpers. Guests vanished and emerged again, making arrangements to leave for other places, only to lose track of one another, hunt around frantically, and discover each other just a short distance away. Around midnight, Tom Buchanan and Mrs. Wilson found themselves confronting each other, arguing passionately about whether Mrs. Wilson had any business speaking Daisy's name.

"Daisy! Daisy! Daisy!" shouted Mrs. Wilson. "I'll say it whenever I want to! Daisy! Dai—"

Making a quick, skillful motion, Tom Buchanan broke her nose with his open hand.

Then there were blood-soaked towels scattered across the bathroom floor, and women's voices raised in scolding tones, and rising above all the chaos came a long, broken cry of agony. Mr. McKee woke up from his nap and stumbled in confusion toward the door. When he reached the halfway point, he turned around and gazed at the chaotic scene—his wife and Catherine both criticizing and comforting as they moved frantically back and forth through the cramped furniture carrying medical supplies, and the desperate figure lying on the couch, bleeding heavily, attempting to spread a copy of Town Tattle over the tapestry depicting scenes of Versailles. Then Mr. McKee turned away and walked out the door. I grabbed my hat from the chandelier and followed him.

"Come have lunch with me sometime," he suggested as we descended in the creaking elevator.

"Where?"

"Anywhere."

"Don't touch the lever," the elevator operator said sharply.

"I'm sorry," said Mr. McKee with dignity, "I didn't realize I was touching it."

"All right," I agreed, "I'll be glad to."

I was standing next to his bed while he sat upright between the sheets, wearing only his underwear, holding a large portfolio in his hands.

"Beauty and the Beast… Loneliness… Old Grocery Horse… Broken Bridge…"

Then I was lying half asleep in the cold lower level of Pennsylvania Station, staring at the morning Tribune, and waiting for the four o'clock train.

Part 3

Throughout the summer nights, music drifted from my neighbor's house. In his blue gardens, men and women came and went like moths among the whispered conversations, champagne, and starlight. During high tide in the afternoons, I would watch his guests dive from his raft's tower or sunbathe on the warm sand of his private beach while his two motorboats cut through the Sound's waters, pulling water-skiers over cascading waves of foam. On weekends, his Rolls-Royce transformed into a shuttle bus, carrying groups of party-goers back and forth between the city from nine in the morning until well after midnight, while his station wagon darted around like an energetic yellow beetle, picking up passengers from every train. Then on Mondays, eight servants, including an additional gardener, worked tirelessly all day with mops, scrub brushes, hammers, and pruning shears, fixing all the damage from the previous night's festivities.

Every Friday, five crates of oranges and lemons would arrive from a fruit vendor in New York—every Monday, these same oranges and lemons would leave through his back door as a pile of squeezed-out halves. In the kitchen stood a machine that could juice two hundred oranges in thirty minutes if a butler pressed a small button two hundred times with his thumb.

At least every two weeks, a team of caterers would arrive with hundreds of feet of canvas and enough colorful lights to turn Gatsby's massive garden into a Christmas tree. On the buffet tables, decorated with gleaming appetizers, spiced baked hams were crowded next to salads arranged in colorful patterns and pastry pigs and turkeys that had been cooked to a rich golden-brown color. In the main hall, they set up a bar with a genuine brass rail and filled it with gins and liquors and with cordials that had been forgotten for so long that most of his female guests were too young to recognize one from another.

By seven o'clock the orchestra has arrived—not some small five-piece group, but a complete ensemble filled with oboes and trombones and saxophones and violins and trumpets and piccolos, along with bass and snare drums. The final swimmers have returned from the beach and are now getting dressed upstairs; cars from New York are lined up five rows deep in the driveway, and the hallways and living rooms and porches are already bright with bold colors, hair cut in striking new styles, and wraps more beautiful than anything from Spain. The bar is bustling with activity, and trays of cocktails circulate through the outdoor garden, filling the air with conversation and laughter, playful hints and introductions immediately forgotten, and excited encounters between women who have never even learned each other's names.

The lights become brighter as the earth moves away from the sun, and now the orchestra plays cheerful cocktail music while the chorus of voices rises to a higher pitch. Laughter comes more easily with each passing moment, flowing freely and generously, sparked by any lighthearted comment. The clusters of people shift more rapidly, growing larger with newcomers, breaking apart and reforming in the same instant; already there are roaming figures, self-assured young women who drift from place to place among the more solid and steady guests, becoming for one brief, delightful moment the focus of a gathering, and then, thrilled by their success, they move on through the ever-changing tide of faces and voices and colors beneath the continuously shifting lights.

Suddenly one of these party guests, dressed in shimmering opal fabric, grabs a cocktail from somewhere nearby, downs it quickly for courage, and moves her hands like a professional dancer as she steps out alone onto the canvas dance floor. A brief silence falls over the crowd; the bandleader accommodates her by adjusting his rhythm, and excited conversation erupts as the false rumor spreads that she's Gilda Gray's backup dancer from the Follies. The party has officially started.

I think that on the first night I attended Gatsby's house party, I was among the few guests who had actually received an invitation. Most people weren't invited—they simply showed up. They climbed into cars that carried them out to Long Island, and somehow they found themselves at Gatsby's front door. Once they arrived, someone who knew Gatsby would introduce them around, and from that point on they behaved according to the casual rules you'd expect at an amusement park. Sometimes people would come and leave without ever meeting Gatsby himself, attending the party with such genuine enthusiasm that their pure enjoyment served as their entry pass.

I had actually received an invitation. A driver dressed in a robin's-egg blue uniform walked across my lawn early that Saturday morning, carrying a remarkably formal note from his boss: the honor would be completely Gatsby's, it stated, if I would come to his "little party" that evening. He had noticed me on several occasions, and had planned to visit me much earlier, but an unusual set of circumstances had stopped him—signed Jay Gatsby, written in an elegant handwriting.

Wearing white flannel clothing, I walked over to his lawn shortly after seven o'clock and wandered around feeling quite uncomfortable among the swirling crowds of people I didn't recognize—although I spotted a few faces I had seen on the commuter train. I was immediately struck by how many young English men were scattered throughout the party; they were all well-dressed, all appeared somewhat eager, and all spoke in quiet, serious tones to wealthy and successful Americans. I felt certain they were trying to sell something: stocks or insurance policies or cars. They were clearly painfully aware of the abundant wealth

45

surrounding them and believed they could claim some of it with just the right words spoken in the proper tone.

As soon as I got there, I tried to locate my host, but the few people I asked about where he was looked at me with such surprise and so strongly insisted they had no idea where he'd gone that I retreated toward the cocktail table—the only spot in the garden where a man by himself could stand around without appearing aimless and lonely.

I was heading off to get completely wasted from pure humiliation when Jordan Baker emerged from the house and positioned herself at the top of the marble steps, tilting slightly backward and gazing down into the garden with scornful curiosity.

Welcome or not, I realized I needed to connect with someone before I could start making friendly comments to people passing by.

"Hello!" I shouted, moving toward her. My voice sounded strangely loud across the garden.

"I thought you might be here," she replied distractedly as I approached. "I remembered you lived next door to—"

She held my hand in a detached way, like a promise that she would attend to me shortly, and listened to two girls wearing matching yellow dresses who had paused at the bottom of the stairs.

"Hello!" they shouted in unison. "Sorry you didn't win."

That was for the golf tournament. She had been defeated in the finals the previous week.

"You don't know who we are," said one of the girls in yellow, "but we met you here about a month ago."

"You've dyed your hair since then," Jordan observed, and I was startled, but the girls had already moved on casually and her comment was directed at the early moon, which appeared like the dinner, undoubtedly from a caterer's basket. With Jordan's slim golden arm linked through mine, we walked down the steps and strolled through the garden. A tray of cocktails drifted toward us in the twilight, and we settled at a table with the two girls dressed in yellow and three men, each introduced to us as Mr. Mumble.

"Do you come to these parties often?" Jordan asked the girl beside her.

"The last one was where I met you," the girl replied, her voice bright and self-assured. She turned to her friend: "Isn't that right, Lucille?"

It was for Lucille, too.

"I enjoy coming here," Lucille said. "I'm never particular about what I do, so I always end up having a wonderful time. The last time I was at one of these parties, I ripped my dress on a chair, and he asked for my name and address—within a week, I received a package from Croirier's containing a brand new evening gown."

"Did you keep it?" asked Jordan.

"Of course I did. I planned to wear it tonight, but it was too large in the chest area and needed alterations. It was gas blue with lavender beads. Two hundred and sixty-five dollars."

"There's something strange about a guy who would do something like that," said the other girl eagerly. "He doesn't want any conflict with anyone."

"Who doesn't?" I asked.

"Gatsby. Somebody told me—"

The two girls and Jordan huddled together, speaking in hushed, secretive tones.

"Someone told me they believed he had killed a man once."

A wave of excitement swept through all of us. The three Mr. Mumbles leaned forward and listened intently.

"I don't think that's really it," Lucille argued skeptically. "It's more likely that he was a German spy during the war."

One of the men nodded in agreement.

"I heard that from someone who knew everything about him and grew up with him in Germany," he told us with complete certainty.

"Oh, no," said the first girl, "that can't be right, because he served in the American army during the war." As we turned our attention back to her, she leaned forward eagerly. "You should watch him sometimes when he thinks no one is looking. I bet he's killed someone."

She squinted and trembled. Lucille trembled too. We all turned around, searching for Gatsby. The fact that people whispered about him—people who had found very little in this world worth whispering about—showed just how much romantic mystery he stirred up in everyone's imagination.

The first dinner—there would be another one after midnight—was now being served, and Jordan invited me to join her group, who were seated around a table on the other side of the garden. There were three married couples and Jordan's date, a relentless college student prone to crude suggestions, and clearly convinced that eventually Jordan would surrender herself to him in some way or another. Rather than wandering around, this group had maintained a respectable unity, and took upon itself the role of representing the established aristocracy of the area—East Egg looking down on West Egg and cautiously protecting itself against its flashy celebration.

"Let's leave," Jordan whispered after a half-hour that felt somehow wasteful and inappropriate; "this is far too polite for me."

We stood up, and she told me that we needed to locate the host: she mentioned that I had never met him before, and this was making me feel uncomfortable. The college student nodded with a cynical, sad expression.

The bar, which we checked first, was packed with people, but Gatsby wasn't there. She couldn't spot him from the top of the stairs, and he wasn't out on the porch either. Taking a chance, we tried a door that looked significant and stepped into a towering Gothic library with walls lined in carved English oak that had likely been shipped over intact from some old estate abroad.

A heavy-set, middle-aged man wearing huge owl-like glasses sat somewhat intoxicated on the edge of a large table, gazing with wavering focus at the rows of books on the shelves. When we walked in, he spun around excitedly and looked Jordan over from top to bottom.

"What do you think?" he asked urgently.

"About what?"

He gestured with his hand toward the bookshelves.

"About that. Actually, you don't need to bother checking. I already checked. They're real."

"The books?"

He nodded.

"Completely real—they have pages and everything. I figured they'd be made of some sturdy cardboard. As it turns out, they're absolutely real. Pages and—Here! Let me show you."

Taking our skepticism as a given, he hurried to the bookshelves and came back with Volume One of the Stoddard Lectures.

"Look!" he shouted with excitement. "It's a real piece of printed material. It completely fooled me. This guy's a genuine Belasco. It's absolutely brilliant. What attention to detail! What authenticity! He knew exactly when to stop too—he didn't even cut the pages. But what more do you want? What did you expect?"

He grabbed the book from my hands and quickly put it back on the shelf, mumbling that if even one book was taken out, the entire library might come crashing down.

"Who brought you here?" he asked. "Or did you come on your own? Someone brought me. Most people were brought by someone else."

Jordan looked at him with alert, cheerful attention, saying nothing in response.

"A woman named Roosevelt brought me here," he went on. "Mrs. Claud Roosevelt. Do you know her? I ran into her somewhere last night. I've been drinking for about a week straight, and I figured sitting in a library might help me sober up."

"Has it?"

"A little bit, I think. I can't tell yet. I've only been here an hour. Did I tell you about the books? They're real. They're—"

"You told us."

We shook hands with him solemnly and returned outside.

The garden's canvas dance floor was now alive with movement; elderly men awkwardly spinning young women in endless, clumsy circles, while sophisticated couples held each other in elaborate, stylish poses as they stayed near the corners—and many unaccompanied women danced alone or temporarily took over from the band to play the banjo or drums. By midnight the festivities had grown more intense. A famous tenor had performed in Italian, and a well-known contralto had sung jazz numbers, and between performances people were putting on "acts" throughout the garden, while joyful, empty bursts of laughter drifted up toward the summer sky. A duo of stage performers, who happened to be the women in yellow, performed a childlike routine in costume, and champagne was poured into glasses larger than finger-bowls. The moon had climbed higher, and floating on the Sound was a triangle of silver ripples, shimmering slightly to the sharp, metallic sound of the banjos on the lawn.

I was still with Jordan Baker. We were sitting at a table with a man around my age and a boisterous young woman who would burst into uncontrollable laughter at the smallest thing. I was having a good time now. I had drunk two glasses of champagne, and the scene before me had transformed into something meaningful, fundamental, and deep.

During a quiet moment in the entertainment, the man looked at me and smiled.

"Your face looks familiar," he said politely. "Didn't you serve in the First Division during the war?"

"Yes, that's right. I served in the Twenty-eighth Infantry."

"I served in the Sixteenth until June 1918. I knew I had seen you somewhere before."

We chatted briefly about some damp, gray little towns in France. Apparently he lived somewhere nearby, because he mentioned that he had just purchased a seaplane and planned to test it out the next morning.

"Want to come with me, old sport? Just near the shore along the Sound."

"What time?"

"Any time that works best for you."

It was on the tip of my tongue to ask his name when Jordan looked around and smiled.

"Are you having a good time now?" she asked.

"Much better." I turned back to my new acquaintance. "This party is quite unusual for me. I haven't even met the host yet. I live over there—" I gestured toward the invisible hedge in the distance, "and this man Gatsby had his chauffeur deliver an invitation to me."

For a moment he stared at me as though he couldn't comprehend what I had said.

"I'm Gatsby," he said suddenly.

"What!" I exclaimed. "Oh, I beg your pardon."

"I thought you knew, old sport. I'm afraid I'm not a very good host."

He smiled with understanding—far more than simple understanding. It was one of those extraordinary smiles that carries a sense of timeless comfort, the kind you might encounter only four or five times in your entire life. For a moment, it seemed to embrace the whole eternal universe, then focused entirely on you with an overwhelming favoritism in your direction. It grasped you exactly as much as you wished to be grasped, had faith in you the way you longed to have faith in yourself, and convinced you that it saw you precisely as you hoped to be seen at your very best. Right at that moment it disappeared—and I found myself looking at a refined young tough guy, a year or two past thirty, whose overly formal way of speaking barely avoided being ridiculous. Even before he told me his name, I had gotten a clear sense that he was choosing his words very deliberately.

Almost the instant Mr. Gatsby revealed who he was, a butler rushed over to inform him that Chicago was on the telephone. He politely excused himself with a slight bow that acknowledged each of us individually.

"If you need anything, just ask for it, old sport," he encouraged me. "Excuse me. I'll come back and join you later."

When he left, I immediately turned to Jordan—feeling compelled to express my astonishment. I had anticipated that Mr. Gatsby would be a ruddy-faced and heavyset man in middle age.

"Who is he?" I asked. "Do you know?"

"He's just a man named Gatsby."

"Where is he from, I mean? And what does he do?"

"Now you've brought up the topic," she replied with a pale smile. "Well, he mentioned to me once that he was an Oxford man."

A faint backdrop began to form behind him, but when she spoke again, it disappeared.

"However, I don't believe it."

"Why not?"

"I don't know," she insisted, "I just don't think he went there."

Something in her tone brought back the other girl's words: "I think he killed a man," and it sparked my curiosity even more. I would have easily believed any story about Gatsby coming from the Louisiana swamplands or the rough neighborhoods of New York's lower East Side. That would have made sense to me. But young men didn't just—at least according to my limited, small-town experience—casually appear out of thin air and purchase a mansion on Long Island Sound.

"Anyway, he throws big parties," Jordan said, switching topics with the kind of sophisticated discomfort city people feel when things get too specific. "And I love big parties. They feel so personal and close. At small parties, you can't get any privacy."

There was the deep thud of a bass drum, and the orchestra leader's voice suddenly cut through the echoing chatter of the garden.

"Ladies and gentlemen," he announced. "At Mr. Gatsby's request, we're going to perform Mr. Vladimir Tostoff's newest composition for you, which caused quite a stir at Carnegie Hall last May. If you follow the news, you'll know it created a major sensation." He grinned with cheerful superiority and added: "What a sensation!" At that, everyone burst into laughter.

"The piece is known," he concluded with enthusiasm, "as 'Vladimir Tostoff's Jazz History of the World!'"

The nature of Mr. Tostoff's composition escaped me, because right as it started my attention turned to Gatsby, standing by himself on the marble steps and glancing from one group to another with satisfied eyes. His bronzed skin was pulled handsomely tight across his face and his short hair appeared as if it were cut every day. I could detect nothing threatening about him. I wondered if the fact that he wasn't drinking helped to separate him from his guests, because it seemed to me that he became more proper as the brotherly merriment grew louder. When the "Jazz History of the World" ended, girls were resting their heads on men's shoulders in a playful, friendly manner, girls were leaning backward teasingly into men's arms, even into groups, confident that someone would catch their falls—but no one leaned backward on Gatsby, and no French bob brushed against Gatsby's shoulder, and no singing quartets formed with Gatsby's head as one member.

"I beg your pardon."

Gatsby's butler suddenly appeared next to us.

"Miss Baker?" he asked. "Excuse me, but Mr. Gatsby would like to speak with you privately."

"With me?" she exclaimed in surprise.

"Yes, madame."

She stood up slowly, lifting her eyebrows at me in surprise, and walked behind the butler toward the house. I observed that she wore her evening gown, and all her dresses, like athletic wear—there was a lively confidence in the way she moved, as if she had originally learned to walk on golf courses during fresh, clear mornings.

I was by myself and it was nearly two o'clock. For quite a while, puzzling and mysterious sounds had been coming from a long room with many windows that hung over the terrace. Avoiding Jordan's college friend, who was currently having an intimate conversation with two chorus girls and who begged me to come over, I went inside.

The large room was packed with people. One of the girls wearing yellow was at the piano, and next to her stood a tall, red-haired young woman from a well-known chorus who was singing. She had consumed quite a bit of champagne, and as she performed, she had clumsily concluded that everything was deeply, deeply melancholy—she wasn't just singing, she was crying as well. Every time there was a break in the song, she filled the silence with ragged, breathless sobs, then resumed the lyrics in a trembling soprano voice. Tears streamed down her face—though not smoothly, because when they touched her heavily mascara-laden eyelashes, they turned black and continued their journey down her cheeks in slow, dark streams. Someone jokingly suggested she should sing the musical notes written on her face, at which point she threw her hands up, collapsed into a chair, and fell into a deep, wine-induced sleep.

"She got into a fight with a man who claims to be her husband," a girl standing next to me explained.

I glanced around the room. Most of the women who remained were now arguing with men who were supposedly their husbands. Even Jordan's group, the four people from East Egg, had been torn apart by conflict. One of the men was speaking with strange intensity to a young actress, and his wife, after trying to laugh off the situation in a composed and detached manner, completely fell apart and turned to indirect tactics—every so often she would suddenly appear beside him like a furious diamond, whispering harshly into his ear: "You promised!"

The reluctance to go home wasn't limited to wayward men alone. The hall was currently occupied by two disappointingly sober men and their extremely indignant wives. The wives were offering each other sympathy in somewhat elevated voices.

"Whenever he sees I'm having a good time he wants to go home."

"I've never heard anything so selfish in my entire life."

"We're always the first ones to leave."

"So are we."

"Well, we're almost the last ones here tonight," one of the men said sheepishly. "The orchestra left half an hour ago."

Despite the wives agreeing that such cruelty was impossible to believe, the argument concluded with a brief fight, and both women were carried away, struggling and kicking, into the darkness.

As I stood in the hall waiting for my hat, the library door opened and Jordan Baker and Gatsby emerged together. He was speaking some final words to her, but the enthusiasm in his demeanor suddenly shifted to stiff formality when several people came over to bid him farewell.

Jordan's friends were calling to her impatiently from the porch, but she stayed a moment longer to shake hands.

"I just heard the most incredible thing," she whispered. "How long were we in there?"

"Why, about an hour."

"It was... simply amazing," she said again, seeming lost in thought. "But I promised I wouldn't share it, and here I am teasing you with it." She yawned elegantly right in front of me. "Please come visit me... Check the phone book... Look under Mrs. Sigourney Howard... That's my aunt..." She was rushing away as she spoke—her tanned hand gave a cheerful wave goodbye as she disappeared back into her group at the doorway.

Feeling quite embarrassed that I had remained so late on my first visit, I made my way over to the remaining guests who had gathered around Gatsby. I was eager to explain that I had been looking for him earlier in the evening and to say sorry for not recognizing him when we met in the garden.

"Don't mention it," he urged me enthusiastically. "Don't give it another thought, old sport." The familiar phrase carried no more genuine warmth than the hand that gave my shoulder a reassuring pat. "And don't forget we're going up in the seaplane tomorrow morning at nine o'clock."

Then the butler, standing behind his shoulder:

"Philadelphia wants you on the phone, sir."

"All right, in a minute. Tell them I'll be right there... Good night."

"Good night."

"Good night." He smiled—and suddenly it felt meaningful to be among the last ones leaving, as though he had wanted it that way all along. "Good night, old sport... Good night."

But as I walked down the steps I saw that the evening wasn't quite finished. Fifty feet from the door a dozen headlights lit up a strange and chaotic scene. In the ditch beside the road, right side up, but violently stripped of one wheel, sat a new coupé that had left Gatsby's driveway not two minutes earlier. The sharp edge of a wall explained how the wheel had been torn off, which was now receiving considerable attention from half a dozen curious chauffeurs. However, since they had left their cars blocking the road, a harsh, discordant noise from those stuck in the back had been audible for some time, and added to the already violent confusion of the scene.

A man wearing a long coat had gotten out of the wrecked car and now stood in the center of the road, glancing back and forth between the vehicle and the tire, then from the tire to the people watching, with a pleasant but confused expression.

"Look!" he said. "It went into the ditch."

The fact was incredibly amazing to him, and I first noticed his extraordinary sense of wonder, and then I recognized the man—it was the former patron of Gatsby's library.

"How did it happen?"

He shrugged his shoulders.

"I don't know anything at all about mechanics," he said with certainty.

"But how did it happen? Did you run into the wall?"

"Don't ask me," said Owl Eyes, washing his hands of the whole matter. "I know very little about driving—next to nothing. It happened, and that's all I know."

"Well, if you're a poor driver you shouldn't try driving at night."

"But I wasn't even trying," he said with indignation, "I wasn't even trying."

A stunned silence came over the onlookers.

"Do you want to kill yourself?"

"You're lucky it was just a wheel! A bad driver and not even trying!"

"You don't understand," the criminal explained. "I wasn't the one driving. There's another man in the car."

The shock that followed this announcement erupted in a prolonged "Ah-h-h!" as the coupé door swung slowly open. The crowd—it had become a crowd now—instinctively stepped backward, and when the door had opened completely there was an eerie silence. Then, very slowly, piece by piece, a pale, limp figure emerged from the wreckage, feeling around cautiously on the ground with a large, unsteady dress shoe.

Blinded by the bright headlights and disoriented by the constant honking of car horns, the ghostly figure stood unsteadily for a moment before he noticed the man wearing the long coat.

"What's the matter?" he asked calmly. "Did we run out of gas?"

"Look!"

Half a dozen fingers pointed at the severed wheel—he stared at it for a moment, then looked up as if he suspected it had fallen from the sky.

"It came off," someone explained.

He nodded.

"At first I didn't notice we'd stopped."

A pause. Then, taking a deep breath and squaring his shoulders, he said in a resolute voice:

"Could you tell me where there's a gas station?"

At least twelve men, some of them slightly better off than he was, explained to him that the wheel and car were no longer connected by any physical link.

"Back out," he suggested after a moment. "Put her in reverse."

"But the wheel's off!"

He hesitated.

"No harm in trying," he said.

The blaring horns had reached their peak and I turned away and walked across the lawn toward home. I looked back once. A thin slice of moon was shining over Gatsby's house, making the night beautiful as it had been before, and outlasting the laughter and the sounds from his still brightly lit garden. A sudden emptiness seemed to pour from the windows and the large doors, surrounding the host with complete loneliness as he stood on the porch, his hand raised in a formal gesture of goodbye.

Looking back at what I've written up to this point, I realize I've created the impression that the events from three separate nights, spaced weeks apart, were the only things that captivated my attention. In reality, these were simply random incidents in a busy summer, and until much later, they occupied my thoughts far less than my own personal matters.

Most of the time I worked. In the early morning the sun cast my shadow westward as I rushed down the white canyons of lower New York to the Probity Trust. I knew the other clerks and young bond salesmen by their first names, and ate lunch with them in dim, packed restaurants where we had small pork sausages and mashed potatoes and coffee. I even had a brief relationship with a girl who lived in Jersey City and worked in the accounting department, but her brother started giving me hostile looks, so when she went on her vacation in July I let it fade quietly away.

I typically ate dinner at the Yale Club—for some reason it was the most depressing part of my day—and afterward I would go upstairs to the library and spend a dedicated hour studying investments and securities. There were usually some rowdy members hanging around, but they never entered the library, so it provided an excellent place to work. Following that, if the evening was pleasant, I would walk down Madison Avenue past the old Murray Hill Hotel, and across 33rd Street to Pennsylvania Station.

I started to fall in love with New York, its vibrant and thrilling atmosphere after dark, and the contentment that came from watching the endless stream of people and vehicles that satisfied my restless gaze. I enjoyed strolling down Fifth Avenue and selecting romantic women from the masses, imagining that within moments I would become part of their world, and nobody would ever find out or judge me. At times, in my imagination, I would follow them to their apartments on the edges of secluded streets, and they would turn around and give me a smile before disappearing through a doorway into cozy shadows. During the magical urban twilight, I sometimes experienced a deep sense of isolation, and I recognized it in others as well—unfortunate young office workers who lingered outside shop windows, killing time until it was appropriate to have dinner alone at a restaurant—young employees in the evening light, squandering the most emotionally charged moments of nighttime and existence.

Again at eight o'clock, when the dark streets of the Forties were packed five rows deep with rumbling taxicabs heading toward the theater district, I felt my heart sink. People leaned close together in the taxis as they waited, voices sang out, and laughter erupted from jokes I couldn't hear, while lit cigarettes traced mysterious patterns in the darkness. Imagining that I was also rushing toward joy and sharing in their private excitement, I wished them well.

For a while I lost track of Jordan Baker, but then in midsummer I ran into her again. At first I felt honored to spend time with her, since she was a golf champion and everyone recognized her name. Then it became something deeper. I wasn't truly in love, but I experienced a kind of gentle fascination. The indifferent, arrogant expression she showed the world was hiding something—most pretenses eventually hide something, even if they don't at first—and one day I discovered what it was. When we attended a house party together up in Warwick, she left a borrowed car outside in the rain with the convertible top down, then lied about it—and suddenly I recalled the story about her that had escaped me that evening at Daisy's. At her first major golf tournament there was a controversy that almost made it into the newspapers—an allegation that she had moved her ball from a difficult position during the semifinal round. The matter nearly became a full-blown scandal—then faded away. A caddy took back his testimony, and the only other witness acknowledged that he could have been wrong. The episode and her name had stayed linked in my memory.

Jordan Baker naturally stayed away from intelligent, perceptive men, and now I understood this was because she felt more secure in situations where breaking the rules seemed unthinkable. She was hopelessly dishonest. She couldn't stand being in a position of weakness and, considering this refusal, I imagine she started using deception when she was quite young to maintain that calm, arrogant smile she showed the world while still meeting the needs of her tough, confident body.

It didn't matter to me. You never really hold dishonesty against a woman too harshly—I felt briefly sorry about it, then put it out of my mind. During that same house party, we had an odd conversation about driving. It began when she drove so close to some workers that our car's fender brushed against a button on one of the men's coats.

"You're a terrible driver," I protested. "Either you should be more careful, or you shouldn't drive at all."

"I am careful."

"No, you're not."

"Well, other people are," she said casually.

"What does that have to do with it?"

"They'll stay out of my way," she insisted. "It takes two people to cause an accident."

"Imagine you encountered someone who was just as reckless as you are."

"I hope I never will," she replied. "I can't stand careless people. That's why I like you."

Her gray, sun-weary eyes looked straight ahead, but she had intentionally changed the dynamic between us, and for a brief moment I thought I was in love with her. However, I think slowly and I'm governed by internal principles that hold back my impulses, and I realized that first I needed to completely untangle myself from that complicated situation back home. I had been sending letters every week and ending them with "Love, Nick," and all I could focus on was how, whenever that particular girl played tennis, a thin line of sweat would form above her upper lip. Still, there was an unspoken agreement that needed to be delicately ended before I could be free.

Everyone believes they possess at least one of the fundamental virtues, and this is mine: I am among the few truly honest people I have ever encountered.

———————————

Part 4

On Sunday morning, while church bells chimed in the villages along the shore, the world and its mistress came back to Gatsby's house and sparkled joyfully across his lawn.

"He's a bootlegger," said the young women, moving somewhere between his cocktails and his flowers. "One time he killed a man who had discovered that he was Von Hindenburg's nephew and second cousin to the devil. Hand me a rose, honey, and pour me one last drop into that crystal glass."

I once jotted down the names of Gatsby's summer guests in the blank margins of a train schedule. The timetable has aged now, falling apart along its creases, with a header that reads "This schedule in effect July 5th, 1922." I can still make out the faded names, and they'll paint a clearer picture than my broad descriptions of the people who enjoyed Gatsby's generous hospitality while offering him the peculiar honor of remaining completely ignorant about who he really was.

From East Egg came the Chester Beckers and the Leeches, along with a man named Bunsen, whom I had known at Yale, and Doctor Webster Civet, who drowned last summer up in Maine. There were also the Hornbeams and the Willie Voltaires, and an entire family called the Blackbucks, who always clustered together in a corner and turned their noses up like goats at anyone who approached them. The Ismays and the Chrysties attended as well (though it was actually Hubert Auerbach and Mr. Chrystie's wife), and Edgar Beaver was there too, whose hair supposedly turned snow-white one winter afternoon for absolutely no reason at all.

Clarence Endive was from East Egg, if I recall correctly. He showed up just once, wearing white knickerbockers, and got into a fight with some vagrant named Etty in the garden. From further out on the Island came the Cheadles and the O. R. P. Schraeders, along with the Stonewall Jackson Abrams from Georgia, and the Fishguards and the Ripley Snells. Snell was there for three days before he was sent to prison, lying so drunk on the gravel driveway that Mrs. Ulysses Swett's car ran over his right hand. The Dancies showed up as well, and S. B. Whitebait, who was well past sixty, and Maurice A. Flink, and the Hammerheads, and Beluga the tobacco importer, and Beluga's women.

From West Egg came the Poles and the Mulreadys and Cecil Roebuck and Cecil Schoen and Gulick the State senator and Newton Orchid, who ran Films Par Excellence, and Eckhaust and Clyde Cohen and Don S. Schwartz (the son) and Arthur McCarty, all involved with the movie business in some way. And the Catlips and the Bembergs and G. Earl Muldoon, brother to that Muldoon who later killed his wife. Da Fontano the promoter showed up there, and Ed Legros and James B. ("Rot-Gut") Ferret and the De Jongs and Ernest Lilly—they came to gamble, and when Ferret wandered out into the garden it meant he was broke and Associated Traction stock would need to move favorably the next day.

A man named Klipspringer visited so frequently that everyone called him "the boarder"—I'm not sure he had anywhere else to live. Among the theater crowd were Gus Waize and Horace O'Donavan and Lester Myer and George Duckweed and Francis Bull. The New York guests included the Chromes and the Backhyssons and the Dennickers and Russel Betty and the Corrigans and the Kellehers and the Dewars and the Scullys and S. W. Belcher and the Smirkes and the young Quinns, who are divorced now, and Henry L. Palmetto, who took his own life by throwing himself in front of a subway train in Times Square.

Benny McClenahan always showed up with four women. They were never exactly the same people physically, but they looked so much alike that it always felt like they'd been there before. I can't remember their names—Jacqueline, I think, or maybe Consuela, or Gloria or Judy or June, and their last names were either the musical names of flowers and months or the more serious ones of major American business tycoons whose relatives, if you pushed them, they would admit to being.

In addition to all these, I can recall that Faustina O'Brien visited there at least once, along with the Baedeker girls and young Brewer, who lost his nose in the war, and Mr. Albrucksburger with Miss Haag, his fiancée, and Ardita Fitz-Peters and Mr. P. Jewett, who was once head of the American Legion, and Miss Claudia Hip, accompanied by a man rumored to be her chauffeur, and a prince of some sort, whom we nicknamed Duke, and whose real name, if I ever learned it, I've since forgotten.

All these people came to Gatsby's house in the summer.

At nine o'clock one morning in late July, Gatsby's magnificent car bumped up the rough driveway to my door and released a burst of music from its three-note horn.

It was the first time he had visited me, even though I had attended two of his parties, flown in his seaplane, and frequently enjoyed his beach at his insistent invitation.

"Good morning, old sport. You're having lunch with me today and I thought we'd ride up together."

He balanced himself on the dashboard of his car with that resourceful way of moving that's so distinctly American— something that comes, I think, from not doing heavy lifting as young people and, even more so, from the unstructured grace of our anxious, irregular games. This quality kept breaking through his careful mannerisms in the form of restlessness. He was never completely still; there was always a foot tapping somewhere or a hand opening and closing impatiently.

He noticed me gazing admiringly at his car.

"It's beautiful, isn't it, old sport?" He stepped aside to give me a better view. "Haven't you ever seen it before?"

I had seen it. Everyone had seen it. It was a rich cream color, gleaming with nickel, bulging at various points along its enormous length with impressive hatboxes and picnic baskets and toolboxes, and layered with a maze of windshields that reflected multiple suns. Settling back behind several layers of glass in what felt like a green leather greenhouse, we headed toward town.

I had spoken with him maybe six times over the past month and discovered, much to my disappointment, that he didn't have much to say. So my initial impression that he was someone of some vague importance had slowly disappeared, and he had simply become the owner of a fancy roadhouse next door.

And then came that unsettling car ride. We hadn't even made it to West Egg village when Gatsby started trailing off mid-sentence and nervously patting his knee through his caramel-colored suit.

"Listen here, buddy," he suddenly burst out, "what do you really think of me, anyway?"

A little overwhelmed, I started giving the kind of vague, non-committal responses that such a question calls for.

"Well, I'm going to tell you something about my life," he interrupted. "I don't want you to get the wrong idea about me from all these stories you hear."

So he knew about the strange accusations that spiced up the conversations in his halls.

"I'll tell you God's truth." His right hand suddenly commanded divine retribution to wait. "I come from a wealthy family in the Middle West—they're all gone now. I grew up in America but went to school at Oxford, since all my forefathers have received their education there for generations. It's a family tradition."

He glanced at me from the corner of his eye—and I understood why Jordan Baker had thought he was lying. He rushed through the words "educated at Oxford," or mumbled them, or stumbled over them, as if they had troubled him before. And with this uncertainty, his entire story crumbled, and I began to wonder if there might be something slightly menacing about him after all.

"What part of the Midwest?" I asked casually.

"San Francisco."

"I see."

"My entire family passed away, and I inherited a substantial amount of money."

His voice carried a serious tone, as though the memory of that abrupt destruction of an entire family still troubled him deeply. For a brief moment I wondered if he might be joking with me, but one look at his expression told me he was completely sincere.

"After that I lived like a young prince in all the major cities of Europe—Paris, Venice, Rome—gathering precious stones, mainly rubies, hunting large wild animals, doing some painting, creating things just for myself, and attempting to put behind me something deeply tragic that had occurred in my distant past."

I struggled to hold back my disbelieving laughter. The expressions themselves had become so overused and clichéd that they brought to mind nothing more than a turbaned "character" spilling sawdust from every opening as he chased a tiger through the Bois de Boulogne.

"Then the war came, old sport. It was a tremendous relief, and I tried desperately to die, but I seemed to live a charmed life. I accepted a commission as first lieutenant when it started. In the Argonne Forest I led what remained of my machine-gun battalion so far ahead that there was a half-mile gap on both sides of us where the infantry couldn't move forward. We held that position for two days and two nights, one hundred and thirty men with sixteen Lewis guns, and when the infantry finally reached us they discovered the insignia of three German divisions scattered among the heaps of corpses. I was promoted to major, and every Allied government awarded me a medal—even Montenegro, tiny Montenegro down on the Adriatic Sea!"

Little Montenegro! He spoke these words with emphasis and gave them an approving nod, accompanied by his characteristic smile. That smile seemed to understand Montenegro's turbulent past and showed compassion for the courageous battles fought by the Montenegrin people. It fully grasped the series of national events that had inspired this heartfelt gesture from Montenegro's passionate spirit. My disbelief now gave way to complete captivation; it felt like rapidly flipping through a stack of magazines.

He reached into his pocket, and a piece of metal hanging from a ribbon dropped into my palm.

"That's the one from Montenegro."

To my amazement, the object appeared genuine. "Orderi di Danilo," read the circular inscription, "Montenegro, Nicolas Rex."

"Turn it."

"Major Jay Gatsby," I read, "For Valour Extraordinary."

"Here's something else I always keep with me. A memento from my time at Oxford. This photograph was taken in Trinity Quad—the gentleman to my left has since become the Earl of Doncaster."

It was a photograph showing about six young men wearing blazers, casually standing around in an archway that revealed numerous church spires in the background. Gatsby was among them, appearing slightly younger than he did now, holding a cricket bat in his hand.

Then it was all true. I could see the tiger skins blazing with color in his palace along the Grand Canal; I could see him opening a chest filled with rubies, hoping their deep crimson glow would soothe the aching of his shattered heart.

"I'm going to ask something important of you today," he said, putting away his keepsakes with satisfaction, "so I figured you should know a bit about who I am. I didn't want you to assume I was just some random person. The thing is, I often end up around people I don't know because I move from place to place, trying to put the painful experiences behind me." He paused. "You'll find out about it later today."

"At lunch?"

"No, this afternoon. I happened to discover that you're taking Miss Baker to tea."

"Do you mean you're in love with Miss Baker?"

"No, old sport, I'm not. But Miss Baker has kindly consented to speak to you about this matter."

I had no clue what "this matter" was, but I felt more irritated than curious. I hadn't invited Jordan over for tea to talk about Mr. Jay Gatsby. I was certain the request would be something completely ridiculous, and for a moment I regretted ever stepping onto his crowded lawn.

He refused to speak another word. His formal behavior became more pronounced as we approached the city. We drove past Port Roosevelt, where we caught sight of red-banded ocean vessels, and raced along a cobblestone slum bordered by the dim, still-occupied taverns from the tarnished-gold nineteen-hundreds. Then the valley of ashes spread out on either side of us, and I caught a glimpse of Mrs. Wilson working vigorously at the garage pump with breathless energy as we passed by.

With fenders stretched out like wings, we cast light across half of Astoria—just half, because as we weaved between the support columns of the elevated train tracks, I heard the recognizable "jug-jug-spat!" sound of a motorcycle, and a frenzied police officer pulled up beside us.

"All right, old sport," Gatsby called out. We reduced our speed. He pulled a white card from his wallet and waved it in front of the man's eyes.

"You're absolutely right," the police officer agreed, touching the brim of his cap. "I'll recognize you next time, Mr. Gatsby. My apologies!"

"What was that?" I asked. "The picture of Oxford?"

"I once did a favor for the commissioner, and now he sends me a Christmas card every year."

Over the great bridge, with sunlight streaming through the steel beams creating a steady pattern of light and shadow on the moving cars below, with the city rising across the river in white clusters and cube-like buildings all constructed with dreams made from money that carries no scent of its origins. The city viewed from the Queensboro Bridge is always the city experienced for the first time, in its initial untamed promise of all the wonder and beauty that exists in the world.

A dead man passed us in a hearse piled high with flowers, followed by two carriages with their window shades pulled down, and by more cheerful carriages carrying friends. The friends peered out at us with the sorrowful eyes and distinctive short upper lips characteristic of southeastern Europe, and I was pleased that the sight of Gatsby's magnificent car was part of their solemn procession. As we crossed Blackwell's Island, a limousine overtook us, driven by a white chauffeur, in which sat three stylishly dressed Black people, two men and a woman. I laughed out loud as their eyes rolled toward us with proud defiance.

"Anything can happen now that we've slid over this bridge," I thought; "anything at all..."

Even Gatsby could happen, without any particular wonder.

————————————————

At the height of midday's blazing heat, I met Gatsby for lunch in a well-ventilated basement restaurant on Forty-second Street. As I blinked to adjust from the brilliant sunlight outside, I spotted him dimly in the entrance area, engaged in conversation with another man.

"Mr. Carraway, this is my friend Mr. Wolfshiem."

A small, flat-nosed Jewish man lifted his large head and looked at me, with two thick tufts of hair sprouting from each nostril. After a moment, I spotted his small eyes in the dim light.

"—So I took one look at him," said Mr. Wolfshiem, shaking my hand earnestly, "and what do you think I did?"

"What?" I asked politely.

But clearly he wasn't talking to me, because he let go of my hand and turned his attention to Gatsby with his expressive nose.

"I gave the money to Katspaugh and told him: 'Listen, Katspaugh, don't give him a single cent until he keeps his mouth shut.' He closed it right then and there."

Gatsby grabbed both of our arms and led us forward into the restaurant, at which point Mr. Wolfshiem cut off the sentence he had just begun and fell into a dreamy, distracted silence.

"Highballs?" asked the head waiter.

"This is a nice restaurant here," said Mr. Wolfshiem, looking at the presbyterian nymphs on the ceiling. "But I like across the street better!"

"Yes, highballs," Gatsby agreed, and then turned to Mr. Wolfshiem: "It's too hot over there."

"Hot and small—yes," said Mr. Wolfshiem, "but full of memories."

"What place is that?" I asked.

"The old Metropole."

"The old Metropole," Mr. Wolfshiem reflected sadly. "Full of faces that are dead and gone. Full of friends who are gone forever now. I can't forget as long as I live the night they shot Rosy

Rosenthal there. There were six of us at the table, and Rosy had been eating and drinking heavily all evening. When it was nearly morning, the waiter approached him with a strange expression and said that someone wanted to speak with him outside. 'All right,' Rosy said, and started to stand up, but I pulled him back down into his chair.

"'Let those bastards come in here if they want you, Rosy, but don't you dare, so help me, step outside this room.'"

"It was four o'clock in the morning then, and if we had raised the blinds we would have seen daylight."

"Did he go?" I asked innocently.

"Of course he went." Mr. Wolfshiem's nose flashed at me with indignation. "He turned around at the door and said: 'Don't let that waiter take away my coffee!' Then he walked out onto the sidewalk, and they shot him three times in his stomach and drove off."

"Four of them were electrocuted," I said, remembering.

"Five, with Becker." His nostrils flared toward me with interest. "I understand you're looking for a business connection."

The contrast between these two comments was striking. Gatsby responded on my behalf:

"Oh, no," he exclaimed, "this isn't the man."

"No?" Mr. Wolfshiem seemed disappointed.

"This is just a friend. I told you we'd talk about that some other time."

"I beg your pardon," said Mr. Wolfshiem, "I had the wrong man."

A delicious hash was served, and Mr. Wolfshiem, abandoning the nostalgic mood of the old Metropole, started eating with intense precision. His gaze, at the same time, moved very deliberately around the entire room—he finished his survey by turning to examine the people sitting right behind us. I believe that, if I hadn't been there, he would have quickly looked under our own table.

"Listen, old sport," Gatsby said, leaning in my direction, "I'm worried I upset you a bit this morning when we were in the car."

There was that smile again, but this time I resisted it.

"I don't like mysteries," I replied, "and I can't understand why you won't be straightforward and tell me what you're after. Why does everything have to go through Miss Baker?"

"Oh, there's nothing sneaky about it," he reassured me. "Miss Baker is a real athlete, you know, and she would never do anything that wasn't proper."

Suddenly he glanced at his watch, sprang to his feet, and rushed out of the room, leaving me alone with Mr. Wolfshiem at the table.

"He needs to make a phone call," said Mr. Wolfshiem, watching him with his eyes. "Great guy, isn't he? Good-looking and a complete gentleman."

"Yes."

"He's an Oxford man."

"Oh!"

"He went to Oggsford College in England. You know Oggsford College?"

"I've heard of it."

"It's one of the most famous colleges in the world."

"Have you known Gatsby for a long time?" I asked.

"Several years," he replied with satisfaction. "I had the pleasure of meeting him right after the war. But I knew I had found a gentleman of excellent upbringing after speaking with him for an hour. I told myself: 'This is the kind of man you'd want to bring home and introduce to your mother and sister.'" He stopped speaking. "I notice you're looking at my cufflinks."

I hadn't been looking at them, but I did now. They were made up of strangely familiar pieces of ivory.

"Finest specimens of human molars," he told me.

"Welll" I examined them. "That's a very interesting idea."

"Yeah." He rolled his sleeves up beneath his coat. "Yeah, Gatsby's extremely cautious when it comes to women. He wouldn't even glance at a friend's wife."

When the person who had earned this instinctive trust came back to the table and took his seat, Mr. Wolfshiem quickly finished his coffee and stood up.

"I've really enjoyed my lunch," he said, "and I'm going to take off before I overstay my welcome with you two young men."

"Take your time, Meyer," Gatsby said without any enthusiasm. Mr. Wolfshiem lifted his hand in what looked like a blessing.

"You're being very polite, but I'm from a different generation," he declared seriously. "You sit here talking about your sports and your girlfriends and your—" He gestured vaguely to fill in some unspoken word. "As for me, I'm fifty years old, and I won't force my company on you any longer."

As he shook hands and walked away, his tragic nose was quivering. I wondered whether I had said something that might have offended him.

"He gets really emotional sometimes," Gatsby explained. "Today is one of those sentimental days for him. He's quite a character around New York—a regular fixture on Broadway."

"Who is he, anyway, an actor?"

"No."

"A dentist?"

"Meyer Wolfshiem? No, he's a gambler." Gatsby paused, then said calmly: "He's the one who rigged the World Series back in 1919."

"Fixed the World Series?" I repeated.

The thought completely overwhelmed me. I recalled, naturally, that the World Series had been rigged in 1919, but if I had considered it at all I would have considered it as something that simply occurred, the conclusion of some unavoidable sequence. It never crossed my mind that one person could begin to manipulate the trust of fifty million people—with the focused determination of a thief cracking a safe.

"How did he end up doing that?" I asked after a moment.

"He just saw the opportunity."

"Why isn't he in jail?"

"They can't get him, old sport. He's a smart man."

I insisted on paying the bill. When the waiter returned with my change, I spotted Tom Buchanan across the packed room.

"Come with me for a moment," I said. "I need to greet someone."

When Tom spotted us, he leaped to his feet and took several steps toward us.

"Where have you been?" he asked eagerly. "Daisy is furious because you haven't called."

"This is Mr. Gatsby, Mr. Buchanan."

They shook hands quickly, and an awkward, unusual expression of discomfort appeared on Gatsby's face.

"How have you been, anyway?" Tom asked me. "How did you end up coming all the way up here to eat?"

"I've been having lunch with Mr. Gatsby."

I looked over at Mr. Gatsby, but he had already disappeared.

One October day in nineteen seventeen—

(Jordan Baker said that afternoon, sitting up very straight on a straight chair in the tea-garden at the Plaza Hotel)

I was walking from one place to another, sometimes on the sidewalks and sometimes on the grass. I preferred walking on the grass because I was wearing shoes from England that had rubber studs on the bottom that gripped into the soft earth. I was also wearing a new plaid skirt that fluttered slightly in the breeze, and whenever this happened the red, white, and blue flags in front of all the houses stretched out rigid and made a tut-tut-tut-tut sound, as if they disapproved.

The biggest banner and the most expansive lawn belonged to Daisy Fay's house. She had just turned eighteen, making her two years my senior, and she was without question the most sought-after young woman in all of Louisville. She always wore white clothing and drove a small white convertible, while her telephone buzzed constantly throughout the day with eager young officers from Camp Taylor begging for the chance to have her all to themselves that evening. "At least for just one hour!"

When I walked past her house that morning, her white sports car was parked at the curb, and she was sitting in it with a lieutenant I had never met before. They were so absorbed in each other that she didn't notice me until I was five feet away.

"Hello, Jordan," she called unexpectedly. "Please come here."

I felt honored that she wanted to talk with me, since she was the older girl I looked up to the most. She wondered if I was heading to the Red Cross to help make bandages. I confirmed that I was. In that case, could I let them know she wouldn't be able to make it that day? While she spoke, the officer gazed at Daisy in the way every young woman hopes to be looked at at some point, and the romantic nature of that moment has stayed with me ever since. His name was Jay Gatsby, and I wouldn't see him again for more than four years—even when I encountered him on Long Island, I had no idea he was the same person.

That was 1917. By the following year, I had several suitors of my own, and I started competing in tournaments, so I rarely saw Daisy anymore. She hung around with a somewhat older group—when she socialized with anyone at all. Crazy stories were going around about her—like how her mother caught her packing her suitcase one winter evening to travel to New York and say farewell to a soldier who was shipping out overseas. Her family successfully stopped her, but she refused to speak to them for weeks afterward.

Following that incident, she stopped fooling around with soldiers entirely, limiting herself to a handful of flat-footed, nearsighted young men in town who were completely ineligible for military service.

By the following autumn, she was cheerful again, as lively as she had ever been. She made her social debut after the armistice ended, and by February people believed she was engaged to a man from New Orleans. In June she wed Tom Buchanan from Chicago, with greater splendor and ceremony than Louisville had ever witnessed. He arrived with a hundred guests in four private railroad cars, rented an entire floor of the Muhlbach Hotel, and the day before their wedding he presented her with a pearl necklace worth three hundred and fifty thousand dollars.

I was a bridesmaid. I entered her room thirty minutes before the wedding dinner and discovered her sprawled on her bed, looking as beautiful as the June evening in her floral gown—and completely intoxicated. She clutched a bottle of Sauterne in one hand while gripping a letter in the other.

"'Congratulate me," she mumbled. "I've never had a drink before, but oh how I'm enjoying it."

"What's wrong, Daisy?"

I was terrified, I can tell you; I had never encountered a girl like that before.

"Here, sweethearts." She fumbled around in a wastebasket that she had brought with her onto the bed and retrieved the pearl necklace. "Take them downstairs and return them to whoever owns them. Tell them that Daisy has changed her mind. Say: 'Daisy has changed her mind!'"

She started crying—she cried endlessly. I hurried out and found her mother's maid, and we locked the door and got her into a cold bath. She refused to release the letter. She brought it into the bathtub with her and crushed it into a soggy ball, and only allowed me to place it in the soap dish when she realized it was falling apart like snow.

But she didn't speak again. We gave her smelling salts and placed ice on her forehead and helped her back into her dress, and thirty minutes later, when we left the room, the pearls were around her neck and the whole episode was finished. The following day at five o'clock she married Tom Buchanan without even a tremor, and departed on a three-month journey to the South Seas.

I saw them in Santa Barbara when they returned, and I thought I'd never seen a woman so crazy about her husband. If he stepped out of the room for even a moment, she'd glance around nervously and ask: "Where did Tom go?" and wear the most distracted look until she spotted him walking back through the door. She would sit on the sand for hours with his head resting in her lap, running her fingers over his eyes and gazing at him with mysterious joy. It was moving to watch them together—it made you chuckle in a quiet, captivated way. That happened in August. A week after I left Santa Barbara, Tom crashed into a wagon on the Ventura road one evening, and tore off a front wheel of his car. The woman who was with him also made it into the newspapers because her arm was broken—she was one of the housekeepers at the Santa Barbara Hotel.

The following April, Daisy gave birth to her daughter, and the couple spent a year living in France. I encountered them one spring while they were in Cannes, and again later when they were staying in Deauville, before they eventually returned to Chicago to make their permanent home. As you're aware, Daisy became quite well-liked in Chicago society. They associated with a fast-paced social circle, all of them young, wealthy, and reckless, yet she managed to maintain a completely spotless reputation. This might be because she abstains from alcohol. There's a significant benefit to staying sober when you're surrounded by heavy drinkers. You can keep your mouth shut and, what's more, you can carefully plan any minor misconduct of your own so that everyone else is too intoxicated to notice or care. It's possible that Daisy never engaged in romantic affairs at all—though there's something about that voice of hers…

Well, around six weeks ago, she heard Gatsby's name for the first time in years. It happened when I asked you—do you recall?—whether you knew Gatsby from West Egg. After you left for home, she came to my room and woke me up, asking: "Which Gatsby?" When I described him—I was barely awake—she spoke in the most peculiar voice, saying it had to be the man she once knew. Only then did I realize this Gatsby was the same officer who had been in her white car.

When Jordan Baker finished telling me all of this, we had already left the Plaza half an hour earlier and were riding in a horse-drawn carriage through Central Park. The sun had set behind the towering apartment buildings where movie stars lived in the West Fifties, and the bright voices of children, who had gathered on the grass like crickets, drifted up through the warm evening air:

"I'm the Sheik of Araby.

Your love belongs to me.

At night when you're asleep

Into your tent I'll creep—"

"It was a strange coincidence," I said.

"But it wasn't a coincidence at all."

"Why not?"

"Gatsby bought that house so that Daisy would be just across the bay."

Then it hadn't been just the stars he was reaching for on that June night. He became real to me, suddenly freed from the emptiness of his meaningless magnificence.

"He wants to know," Jordan went on, "if you'll invite Daisy to your house some afternoon and then let him come over."

The humble nature of his request stunned me. He had waited five years and purchased a grand estate where he scattered brilliance to wandering moths—all so he could "drop by" some afternoon to a stranger's garden.

"Did I need to know all of this before he could ask for something so small?"

"He's scared because he's been waiting for such a long time. He was worried that you might take offense. You know, deep down he's actually pretty tough."

Something was bothering me.

"Why didn't he ask you to arrange a meeting?"

"He wants her to see his house," she explained. "And your house is right next door."

"Oh!"

"I think he was partly hoping she would show up at one of his parties some evening," Jordan continued, "but she never appeared. After that, he started casually asking people if they knew her, and I was the first person he discovered who did. That was the night he called me over at his party, and you should have heard how carefully he built up to asking about her. Naturally, I right away suggested we arrange a lunch meeting in New York—and I thought he was going to lose his mind:

"'I don't want to do anything unusual!' he kept saying. 'I want to see her right next door.'"

"When I mentioned that you were a close friend of Tom's, he began to give up on the entire plan. He doesn't know much about Tom, although he claims he's been reading a Chicago newspaper for years just hoping to spot Daisy's name."

It was dark by now, and as we passed under a small bridge I wrapped my arm around Jordan's golden shoulder and pulled her closer to me, asking her to have dinner with me. All at once I stopped thinking about Daisy and Gatsby, and instead focused on this straightforward, tough, no-nonsense person who approached everything with complete skepticism, and who leaned back confidently right there in the circle of my arm. A phrase started pounding in my head with an intoxicating thrill: "There are only the pursued, the pursuing, the busy, and the tired."

"And Daisy ought to have something in her life," Jordan murmured to me.

"Does she want to see Gatsby?"

"She shouldn't find out about it. Gatsby doesn't want her to know. You're just supposed to invite her to tea."

We drove past a wall of dark trees, and then the front of Fifty-Ninth Street, a stretch of soft pale light, shone down into the park. Unlike Gatsby and Tom Buchanan, I didn't have a girl whose ghostly face drifted along the shadowy ledges and blazing signs, so I pulled the girl next to me closer, wrapping my arms tighter around her. Her pale, mocking mouth curved into a smile, so I drew her up again, bringing her even closer to my face this time.

When I returned home to West Egg that evening, I thought for a moment that my house might be burning. It was two in the morning, and the entire corner of the peninsula was glowing with bright lights that cast an eerie glow on the bushes and created thin, stretching reflections on the roadside wires. As I turned the corner, I realized the light was coming from Gatsby's house, which was illuminated from top to bottom.

At first I thought it was another party, a wild celebration that had turned into "hide-and-seek" or "sardines" with the entire house open for the game. But there wasn't a sound. Only wind in the trees, which blew against the wires and made the lights flicker on and off as if the house had blinked into the darkness. As my taxi rumbled away I saw Gatsby walking toward me across his lawn.

"Your place looks like the World's Fair," I said.

"Does it?" He looked toward it without really focusing. "I've been looking into some of the rooms. Let's go to Coney Island, old sport. In my car."

"It's too late."

"Well, how about we jump in the swimming pool? I haven't used it all summer."

"I need to go to bed."

"All right."

He waited, watching me with barely contained excitement.

"I spoke with Miss Baker," I said after a moment. "I'm going to call Daisy tomorrow and invite her over for tea."

"Oh, that's fine," he said casually. "I don't want to cause you any inconvenience."

"What day would work for you?"

"What day would work for you?" he quickly corrected himself. "I don't want to cause you any inconvenience, you understand."

"How about the day after tomorrow?"

He thought about it for a moment. Then, hesitantly: "I want to get the grass cut," he said.

We both glanced down at the grass—there was a distinct boundary where my unkempt lawn stopped and his darker, meticulously maintained stretch started. I had a feeling he was referring to my grass.

"There's one more small matter," he said with uncertainty, and he paused.

"Would you rather wait a few days?" I asked.

"Oh, that's not what this is about. At least—" He struggled to find the right words to begin. "Well, I was thinking—listen, old friend, you don't earn much money, do you?"

"Not very much."

This appeared to comfort him, and he went on with greater confidence.

"I thought you didn't, if you'll pardon my—you see, I run a small business on the side, a kind of side operation, you understand. And I thought that if you don't earn very much— You're selling bonds, aren't you, old sport?"

"Trying to."

"Well, this might interest you. It wouldn't take much of your time and you could make some good money. It happens to be a rather confidential matter."

I understand now that if the situation had been different, that conversation could have become one of the turning points in my life. However, since the proposal was clearly and crudely for services to be provided, I had no option but to stop him right there.

"I'm completely swamped," I said. "I really appreciate it, but I can't take on any additional work right now."

"You wouldn't need to have any dealings with Wolfshiem." Clearly he believed that I was avoiding the "connection" he had brought up during lunch, but I told him he was mistaken. He lingered a bit longer, hoping I would start talking, but I was too lost in thought to engage, so he reluctantly headed home.

The evening had left me feeling dizzy and cheerful; I believe I fell into a deep sleep the moment I walked through my front door. So I have no idea whether Gatsby actually went to Coney Island, or how many hours he spent "peering into rooms" while his house glowed brightly in the night. I phoned Daisy from the office the following morning and asked her to come over for tea.

"Don't bring Tom," I warned her.

"What?"

"Don't bring Tom."

"Who is 'Tom'?" she asked innocently.

The day we had planned was drenched with pouring rain. At eleven o'clock, a man wearing a raincoat and pulling a lawn mower knocked on my front door, explaining that Mr. Gatsby had sent him to cut my grass. This made me realize I had forgotten to ask my Finnish housekeeper to return, so I drove to West Egg Village to look for her through the wet, whitewashed alleyways and to purchase cups, lemons, and flowers.

The flowers weren't needed, because at two o'clock a greenhouse delivery arrived from Gatsby's, complete with countless containers to hold everything. An hour later, the front door opened with obvious nervousness, and Gatsby rushed in wearing a white flannel suit, silver shirt, and gold-colored tie. His face was pale, and dark circles under his eyes showed he hadn't been sleeping.

"Is everything all right?" he asked immediately.

"The grass looks fine, if that's what you mean."

"What grass?" he asked, looking confused. "Oh, the grass in the yard." He glanced out the window toward it, but based on the look on his face, I don't think he actually saw anything at all.

"Looks very good," he said absently. "One of the newspapers mentioned they expected the rain to stop around four o'clock. I believe it was The Journal. Do you have everything you need for— for tea?"

I brought him into the pantry, where he glanced somewhat disapprovingly at the Finn. We examined the twelve lemon cakes from the delicatessen together.

"Will they do?" I asked.

"Of course, of course! They're fine!" and he added hollowly, "… old sport."

The rain slowed to a light mist around three-thirty, with scattered droplets drifting through the air like morning dew. Gatsby stared blankly at the pages of Clay's Economics, jumping at every footstep that made the kitchen floor creak, and glancing nervously at the foggy windows as though something troubling but unseen was happening beyond them. Eventually he stood up and told me in a shaky voice that he needed to go home.

"Why's that?"

"Nobody's coming to tea. It's too late!" He glanced at his watch as though he had some urgent appointment waiting for him somewhere else. "I can't wait around all day."

"Don't be silly; it's just two minutes to four."

He sat down miserably, as though I had shoved him, and at the same moment there was the sound of a car engine turning into my driveway. We both leaped to our feet, and feeling somewhat unsettled myself, I walked out into the yard.

Under the dripping bare lilac trees, a large convertible was making its way up the driveway. It came to a stop. Daisy's face, tilted to one side beneath a triangular lavender hat, peered out at me with a brilliant, joyful smile.

"Is this really where you live, my dearest one?"

The thrilling melody of her voice cut through the rain like an intoxicating remedy. I found myself tracking its rhythm for a brief moment, rising and falling, listening with complete attention before I could make out any actual words. A wet strand of hair clung to her cheek like a stroke of blue paint, and when I reached out to help her from the car, her hand was slick with sparkling raindrops.

"Are you in love with me," she whispered quietly in my ear, "or why did I have to come by myself?"

"That's the secret of Castle Rackrent. Tell your driver to go far away and spend an hour."

"Come back in an hour, Ferdie." Then in a serious whisper: "His name is Ferdie."

"Does the gasoline affect his nose?"

"I don't think so," she said innocently. "Why?"

We walked inside. To my complete shock, the living room was empty.

"Well, that's funny," I said.

"What's funny?"

She turned her head when she heard a gentle, respectful knock at the front door. I walked out and opened it. Gatsby stood there, his face as white as a ghost, his hands buried deep in his coat pockets like heavy stones, standing in a pool of water while staring at me with tragic intensity.

With his hands still buried in his coat pockets, he walked past me into the hallway, turned abruptly as though he were moving on a wire, and vanished into the living room. There was nothing amusing about it. Conscious of my heart pounding loudly in my chest, I pulled the door shut against the intensifying rain.

For thirty seconds, complete silence filled the air. Then I caught a muffled, strangled sound coming from the living room, mixed with what might have been part of a laugh, and after that came Daisy's voice with its sharp, forced tone:

"I'm really happy to see you again."

A pause; it lasted terribly long. I had nothing to do in the hallway, so I entered the room.

Gatsby stood leaning against the fireplace mantel with his hands still tucked in his pockets, trying hard to appear completely relaxed and even uninterested, though the effort showed. He had tilted his head back so far that it touched the face of a broken mantelpiece clock, and from there his troubled eyes gazed down at Daisy, who sat perched nervously yet elegantly on the edge of a rigid chair.

"We've met before," Gatsby mumbled. His eyes briefly looked at me, and his lips opened as he tried unsuccessfully to laugh. Fortunately, the clock chose that moment to lean precariously under the weight of his head, so he quickly turned and grabbed it with shaking hands, placing it back where it belonged. Then he sat down stiffly, resting his elbow on the sofa's arm and his chin in his palm.

"I'm sorry about the clock," he said.

My face had turned a deep red from embarrassment. I couldn't come up with even one ordinary thing to say, despite having a thousand thoughts racing through my mind.

"It's an old clock," I said to them foolishly.

I think we all believed for a moment that it had shattered into pieces on the floor.

"We haven't seen each other in many years," Daisy said, her voice as matter-of-fact as it could ever be.

"Five years next November."

The mechanical way Gatsby responded left all of us speechless for at least another minute. I had managed to get both of them standing with my frantic suggestion that they assist me in preparing tea in the kitchen when that devilish Finn carried it in on a tray.

During the pleasant chaos of teacups and pastries, a sense of proper behavior settled over the room. Gatsby positioned himself in a shadowy corner and, as Daisy and I conversed, watched us both intently with strained, miserable eyes. Since staying calm wasn't the ultimate goal, I found an excuse as soon as I could and stood up to leave.

"Where are you going?" Gatsby asked with sudden alarm.

"I'll be back."

"I need to talk to you about something before you leave."

He followed me frantically into the kitchen, shut the door behind him, and whispered "Oh, God!" in a wretched tone.

"What's the matter?"

"This is a terrible mistake," he said, shaking his head from side to side, "a terrible, terrible mistake."

"You're just embarrassed, that's all," and fortunately I added: "Daisy's embarrassed too."

"She's embarrassed?" he repeated in disbelief.

"Just as much as you are."

"Don't talk so loud."

"You're acting like a little boy," I said, my patience finally snapping. "Not only that, but you're being rude. Daisy's sitting in there all by herself."

He lifted his hand to silence me, gave me a look of unforgettable reproach, and carefully opened the door before returning to the other room.

I walked out the back way—just as Gatsby had when he had made his nervous circuit of the house half an hour before—and ran for a huge black knotted tree, whose thick leaves formed a canopy against the rain. Once more it was pouring, and my uneven lawn, well-trimmed by Gatsby's gardener, was filled with small muddy swamps and ancient marshes. There was nothing to look at from under the tree except Gatsby's enormous house, so I stared at it, like Kant at his church steeple, for half an hour. A brewer had built it early in the "period" craze, a decade before, and there was a story that he'd agreed to pay five years' taxes on all the neighboring cottages if the owners would have their roofs thatched with straw. Perhaps their refusal broke his spirit regarding his plan to establish a family dynasty—he went into an immediate decline. His children sold his house with the black wreath still hanging on the door. Americans, while willing, even eager, to be servants, have always been stubborn about being peasants.

After thirty minutes, the sun came out again, and the grocery store owner's car came around Gatsby's driveway carrying the ingredients for his staff's dinner—I was certain he wouldn't touch a bite. A housemaid started opening the upstairs windows of his home, briefly appeared at each one, and leaning out from the big center bay window, thoughtfully spit into the garden below. It was time for me to head back. While the rain had been falling, it seemed like the sound of their conversation, getting louder and more intense occasionally with bursts of feeling. But in this new quiet, I sensed that silence had settled inside the house as well.

I entered the room—after making as much noise as possible in the kitchen, stopping just short of knocking over the stove—but I don't think they heard anything. They sat at opposite ends of the couch, gazing at each other as though a question had been posed, or hung in the air between them, and all traces of awkwardness had vanished. Daisy's face was streaked with tears, and when I walked in she sprang to her feet and started dabbing at her cheeks with her handkerchief in front of a mirror. But the transformation in Gatsby was absolutely bewildering. He practically radiated light; without saying a word or making any triumphant gesture, a fresh sense of happiness emanated from him and flooded the small room.

"Oh, hello, old sport," he said, as though he hadn't seen me in years. For a moment, I thought he was going to shake my hand.

"It's stopped raining."

"Has it?" When he understood what I was referring to, that there were sparkling patches of sunlight in the room, he smiled like a meteorologist, like a delighted enthusiast of returning light, and shared the news with Daisy. "What do you think of that? It's stopped raining."

"I'm glad, Jay." Her voice, thick with painful, sorrowful beauty, revealed only her surprising happiness.

"I want you and Daisy to come over to my house," he said, "I'd like to show her around."

"Are you sure you want me to come?"

"Absolutely, old sport."

Daisy headed upstairs to wash her face—I realized with embarrassment, too late, that I should have thought about the condition of my towels—while Gatsby and I remained waiting on the lawn.

"My house looks good, doesn't it?" he asked. "Look at how the entire front catches the light."

I agreed that it was splendid.

"Yes." His gaze swept across the entire structure, taking in every curved doorway and rectangular tower. "It only took me three years to make the money I needed to buy it."

"I thought you inherited your money."

"I did, old sport," he said automatically, "but I lost most of it in the big panic—the panic of the war."

I think he barely understood what he was saying, because when I asked him what kind of work he did, he replied: "That's my business," before he realized that wasn't a suitable response.

"Oh, I've been involved in several different ventures," he corrected himself. "I worked in the pharmaceutical industry and later moved into the oil business. But I'm not part of either industry anymore." He studied me more carefully. "Are you saying you've been considering what I suggested the other night?"

Before I could respond, Daisy emerged from the house, and two rows of brass buttons on her dress sparkled in the sunlight.

"That enormous place over there?" she exclaimed, pointing.

"Do you like it?"

"I love it, but I don't see how you live there all alone."

"I always keep it filled with fascinating people, day and night. People who do remarkable things. Famous people."

Instead of taking the shortcut along the Sound, we went down to the road and entered through the large back gate. With delightful whispers, Daisy praised this feature or that of the castle-like outline against the sky, praised the gardens, the bright scent of daffodils and the light, airy scent of hawthorn and plum blossoms and the soft golden scent of the flowering shrubs. It felt odd to reach the marble steps and find no movement of colorful dresses going in and out of the door, and hear no sound except bird songs in the trees.

As we walked through the music rooms that belonged to Marie Antoinette and the Restoration-era salons, I had the feeling that guests were hiding behind every piece of furniture—couches and tables alike—instructed to hold their breath in complete silence until we moved on. When Gatsby shut the door to what he called "the Merton College Library," I could have sworn I heard the man with owl-like eyes burst into eerie laughter.

We climbed the stairs, passing through historic bedrooms draped in rose and lavender silk and brightened with fresh flowers, moving through dressing rooms and billiard rooms, and bathrooms featuring sunken tubs—stepping into one room where a disheveled man in pajamas was performing liver exercises on the floor. This was Mr. Klipspringer, the "boarder." I had noticed him wandering around the beach hungrily that morning. Eventually we reached Gatsby's personal quarters, consisting of a bedroom and bathroom, plus an Adam-style study, where we settled down and enjoyed a glass of Chartreuse that he retrieved from a wall cabinet.

He never stopped watching Daisy, and I believe he was reassessing everything in his home based on how she reacted to it with those cherished eyes of hers. At times, he would also gaze around at his belongings with a bewildered expression, as if her incredible presence there made none of it feel real anymore. At one point he almost fell down a staircase.

His bedroom was the most basic room in the house—except for the dresser, which was decorated with a complete grooming set made of pure matte gold. Daisy picked up the brush with pleasure and smoothed her hair, and then Gatsby sat down, covered his eyes with his hand, and started to laugh.

"It's the funniest thing, old sport," he said with laughter. "I can't—When I try to—"

He had clearly gone through two different emotional states and was now moving into a third. Following his initial awkwardness and his irrational happiness, he was now overwhelmed with amazement at seeing her there. He had been completely absorbed by this idea for such a long time, had imagined every detail from beginning to end, and had waited with clenched determination at an unimaginable level of intensity. Now, as the tension released, he was winding down like a clock that had been wound too tightly.

Recovering himself in a moment, he opened two massive patent cabinets for us that contained his collection of suits, dressing gowns, and ties, along with his shirts, stacked like bricks in piles twelve high.

"I have a man in England who buys my clothes for me. He sends over a selection of items at the beginning of each season, spring and fall."

He pulled out a stack of shirts and started tossing them, one after another, in front of us, shirts made of transparent linen and heavy silk and delicate flannel, which lost their creases as they dropped and spread across the table in a colorful mess. As we watched in amazement, he brought out more, and the soft luxurious pile grew taller—shirts with stripes and decorative patterns and checkered designs in coral and apple-green and lavender and pale orange, with monograms in deep blue. All at once, with a choked noise, Daisy buried her face in the shirts and started sobbing uncontrollably.

"They're such beautiful shirts," she sobbed, her voice muffled in the thick folds. "It makes me sad because I've never seen such—such beautiful shirts before."

After touring the house, we were supposed to see the grounds and the swimming pool, along with the seaplane and the midsummer flowers—but outside Gatsby's window it started raining again, so we lined up looking at the rippled surface of the Sound.

"If it wasn't for the fog, we could see your house on the other side of the bay," Gatsby said. "There's always a green light glowing all night long at the end of your pier."

Daisy suddenly linked her arm through his, but he appeared lost in thought about what he had just expressed. Perhaps he had realized that the enormous meaning of that light had now disappeared forever. When measured against the vast gap that had once existed between him and Daisy, the light had appeared very close to her, nearly within reach. It had felt as near as a star is to the moon. Now it was simply a green light on a pier once more. The number of magical things in his world had decreased by one.

I started walking around the room, looking at various unclear objects in the dim light. A large photograph of an elderly man in sailing clothes caught my attention, hanging on the wall above his desk.

"Who's this?"

"That? That's Mr. Dan Cody, old sport."

The name sounded somewhat familiar.

"He's dead now. He used to be my best friend years ago."

There was a small photograph of Gatsby on the dresser, also dressed in sailing clothes—Gatsby with his head tilted back in a defiant pose—apparently taken when he was around eighteen years old.

"I love it," Daisy exclaimed. "The pompadour! You never told me you had a pompadour—or a yacht."

"Look at this," Gatsby said quickly. "Here are a bunch of newspaper clippings—about you."

They stood next to each other, looking it over. I was about to ask if I could see the rubies when the telephone rang, and Gatsby picked up the receiver.

"Yes… Well, I can't talk right now… I can't talk right now, old sport… I said a small town… He must understand what a small town is… Well, he's of no use to us if Detroit is what he considers a small town…"

He hung up the phone.

"Come here quickly!" Daisy called out from the window.

The rain continued to fall, but the darkness had lifted in the west, and a pink and golden mass of billowing, foamy clouds stretched above the ocean.

"Look at that," she whispered, and then after a moment: "I'd like to just get one of those pink clouds and put you in it and push you around."

I attempted to leave at that point, but they refused to let me go; maybe having me there made their solitude feel more complete and satisfying.

"I know what we'll do," said Gatsby, "we'll have Klipspringer play the piano."

He left the room shouting "Ewing!" and came back a few minutes later with an embarrassed, somewhat tired-looking young man who wore shell-rimmed glasses and had thin blond hair. He was now properly dressed in a casual shirt with an open collar, sneakers, and canvas pants in an indistinct color.

"Did we interrupt your workout?" Daisy asked politely.

"I was asleep," Mr. Klipspringer exclaimed, suddenly flustered with embarrassment. "Well, I mean I had been sleeping. Then I woke up..."

"Klipspringer plays the piano," said Gatsby, cutting him off. "Don't you, Ewing, old sport?"

"I don't play well. I don't—I hardly play at all. I'm completely out of practice—"

"We'll go downstairs," Gatsby cut in. He flipped a switch. The gray windows vanished as the house filled with bright light.

In the music room, Gatsby switched on a single lamp next to the piano. He used a shaking match to light Daisy's cigarette, then settled beside her on a sofa positioned far across the room, where the only illumination came from light reflecting off the polished floor from the hallway.

When Klipspringer finished playing "The Love Nest," he turned around on the bench and looked through the darkness, searching unhappily for Gatsby.

"I'm completely out of practice, you see. I told you I couldn't play. I'm completely out of prac—"

"Don't talk so much, old sport," Gatsby ordered. "Play!"

"In the morning,

In the evening,

Ain't we got fun—"

Outside, the wind howled loudly and a distant rumble of thunder rolled across the Sound. All the lights were beginning to flicker on throughout West Egg; the electric trains, packed with commuters, were rushing home through the rain from New York. This was the time of deep human transformation, and anticipation was building in the atmosphere.

"One thing's certain and nothing's more certain

The rich get richer and the poor get—children.

In the meantime,

In between time—"

As I walked over to say goodbye, I noticed that the confused expression had returned to Gatsby's face, as if a slight uncertainty had crossed his mind about how good his current happiness really was. Nearly five years! There must have been times even that afternoon when Daisy fell short of his expectations—not because of anything she did wrong, but because his fantasy about her was so incredibly powerful. His illusion had grown beyond her, beyond everything else. He had poured himself into it with passionate creativity, constantly building it up, decorating it with every beautiful detail that came his way. Nothing real or new can compete with what a man can build up in the hidden depths of his heart.

As I observed him, he made a slight, noticeable adjustment to his posture. His hand grasped hers, and when she whispered something quietly in his ear, he turned toward her with a sudden surge of feeling. I believe it was her voice that captivated him most, with its shifting, passionate intensity, because it was impossible to imagine anything more beautiful—that voice was an eternal melody.

They had forgotten about me, but Daisy looked up and extended her hand toward me; Gatsby didn't recognize me at all anymore. I glanced at them one final time and they returned my gaze, distantly, consumed by their passionate connection. Then I left the room and walked down the marble steps into the rain, leaving the two of them there together.

Part 6

About this time an ambitious young reporter from New York showed up one morning at Gatsby's door and asked him if he had anything to say.

"Anything to say about what?" Gatsby asked politely.

"Why—any statement to give out."

After five confusing minutes, it became clear that the man had heard Gatsby's name mentioned around his office in some context that he either wouldn't explain or didn't completely grasp. This was his day off, and with admirable initiative, he had rushed out "to see."

It was a lucky guess, but the reporter's gut feeling proved correct. Gatsby's fame, fueled by the hundreds of people who had enjoyed his parties and therefore considered themselves experts on his background, had grown throughout the summer until he was almost newsworthy. Modern myths like the "secret smuggling route to Canada" became linked to his name, and one stubborn rumor claimed he didn't actually live in a house at all, but rather on a boat disguised as a house that was secretly moved back and forth along the Long Island coastline. Exactly why these made-up stories brought satisfaction to James Gatz from North Dakota is difficult to explain.

James Gatz—that was his real name, or at least his legal one. He changed it when he was seventeen, at the exact moment his career began—the moment he watched Dan Cody's yacht anchor in the most dangerous shallows of Lake Superior. James Gatz had been wandering along the beach that afternoon wearing a ripped green jersey and canvas pants, but it was Jay Gatsby who borrowed a rowboat, rowed out to the Tuolomee, and warned Cody that the wind could catch his yacht and destroy it within half an hour.

I imagine he had been holding onto that name for quite some time, even back then. His parents were lazy and failed farmers—his imagination had never truly acknowledged them as his real parents. The reality was that Jay Gatsby of West Egg, Long Island, emerged from his idealized vision of himself. He was a child of God—a description that, if it has any meaning at all, means exactly that—and he needed to pursue His Father's work, serving a grand, crude, and flashy kind of beauty. Therefore, he created precisely the kind of Jay Gatsby that any seventeen-year-old would likely dream up, and he remained devoted to this vision until the very end.

For more than a year, he had been making his way along the southern shore of Lake Superior, working as a clam digger and salmon fisherman, or taking on whatever job would provide him with food and shelter. His tanned, strengthening body thrived naturally in the demanding yet leisurely work of those invigorating days. He encountered women at an early age, and because they pampered him, he grew to look down on them—on young unmarried women for their naivety, and on the experienced ones for their emotional outbursts over matters that, in his complete self-centeredness, he considered ordinary.

His heart remained in constant, chaotic turmoil. The most bizarre and outlandish fantasies plagued him in bed each night. A world of indescribable extravagance unfolded in his mind while the clock ticked away on the washstand and moonlight drenched his crumpled clothes scattered across the floor with its pale glow. Every night he expanded the elaborate tapestry of his daydreams until sleepiness descended upon some brilliant vision with a forgetful embrace. For a time these fantasies served as an escape for his creativity; they offered a convincing suggestion that reality itself was unreal, a guarantee that the solid foundation of the world rested safely upon a fairy's delicate wing.

An instinct toward his future glory had driven him, several months earlier, to the small Lutheran College of St. Olaf's in southern Minnesota. He remained there for two weeks, appalled by its brutal indifference to the beating drums of his destiny, to destiny itself, and loathing the janitorial work he was supposed to do to pay his way through school. Then he wandered back to Lake Superior, and he was still looking for something to do on the day that Dan Cody's yacht dropped anchor in the shallow waters near the shore.

Cody was fifty years old at that time, shaped by the Nevada silver mines, the Yukon, and every metal rush since 1875. The copper deals in Montana that made him a multimillionaire many times over left him physically strong but mentally declining, and sensing this vulnerability, countless women attempted to take his money from him. The unsavory schemes through which Ella Kaye, the newspaper reporter, manipulated his weakness like Madame de Maintenon and convinced him to go to sea on a yacht became widely known through the sensational press coverage of 1902. He had been sailing along overly welcoming coastlines for five years when he appeared as James Gatz's fate in Little Girl Bay.

To the young Gatz, resting on his oars and gazing up at the railed deck, that yacht embodied all the beauty and glamour the world had to offer. I imagine he flashed a smile at Cody—he had likely learned that people were drawn to him when he smiled. In any case, Cody questioned him briefly (one of these questions brought forth the brand new name) and discovered that he was sharp and wildly ambitious. Several days later, he brought him to Duluth and purchased him a blue coat, six pairs of white duck trousers, and a yachting cap. And when the Tuolomee departed for the West Indies and the Barbary Coast, Gatsby departed as well.

He worked in an unclear personal role—during his time with Cody, he served as steward, first mate, captain, secretary, and sometimes even a guard, because Dan Cody when sober understood what extravagant behavior Dan Cody when drunk was capable of, so he dealt with these situations by placing increasing confidence in Gatsby. This arrangement continued for five years, during which their yacht sailed around the continent three times. It could have gone on forever if not for Ella Kaye boarding the vessel one evening in Boston, and Dan Cody's untimely death just one week afterward.

I recall the picture of him hanging in Gatsby's bedroom, a gray-haired, ruddy-faced man with a harsh, vacant expression—the original libertine, who during a particular era of American history brought the brutal savagery of frontier brothels and saloons back to the East Coast. Gatsby's minimal drinking was indirectly Cody's influence. Occasionally during lively parties women would pour champagne over his hair; but he himself had developed the practice of avoiding alcohol entirely.

Cody left him money in his will—twenty-five thousand dollars. But he never received it. He couldn't grasp the legal maneuver that worked against him, though whatever was left of those millions went untouched to Ella Kaye. What he was left with was his uniquely fitting education; the unclear outline of Jay Gatsby had developed into the reality of a complete person.

He shared all of this with me much later, but I'm including it here to dispel those early wild rumors about his background, which weren't even remotely accurate. Furthermore, he revealed this information to me during a period of uncertainty, when I had come to the point of believing both everything and nothing about him. So I'm using this brief pause, while Gatsby, in a sense, gathered himself, to clear away these misunderstandings.

It was also a pause in my involvement with his business matters. For several weeks I didn't encounter him or hear his voice over the telephone—I spent most of my time in New York, running around with Jordan and attempting to win favor with her elderly aunt—but eventually I visited his house one Sunday afternoon. I had barely been there two minutes when someone escorted Tom Buchanan inside for a drink. I was shocked, of course, but what truly amazed me was that this hadn't occurred earlier.

They were a group of three people on horseback—Tom and a man named Sloane and a beautiful woman in a brown riding outfit, who had been there before.

"I'm thrilled to see you," said Gatsby, standing on his porch. "I'm so glad you stopped by."

As if they actually cared!

"Sit right down. Have a cigarette or a cigar." He walked around the room quickly, ringing bells. "I'll have something to drink for you in just a minute."

He was deeply moved by Tom's presence there. However, he would remain uncomfortable until he had offered them something, understanding in some unclear way that this was the only reason for their visit. Mr. Sloane didn't want anything. Perhaps some lemonade? No, thank you. Maybe a bit of champagne? Nothing at all, thanks… I apologize—

"Did you have a nice ride?"

"Very good roads around here."

"I suppose the cars—"

"Yeah."

Driven by an overwhelming urge, Gatsby turned toward Tom, who had received the introduction as if he were meeting someone completely new.

"I believe we've met somewhere before, Mr. Buchanan."

"Oh, yes," said Tom, roughly polite, but clearly not remembering. "So we did. I remember very well."

"About two weeks ago."

"That's right. You were with Nick here."

"I know your wife," Gatsby continued, his tone almost aggressive.

"Is that so?"

Tom turned to me.

"You live near here, Nick?"

"Next door."

"Is that so?"

Mr. Sloane didn't join the conversation, but instead leaned back arrogantly in his chair; the woman remained silent as well—until suddenly, after two drinks, she became friendly.

"We'll all come to your next party, Mr. Gatsby," she suggested. "What do you say?"

"Absolutely; I'd be thrilled to have you join me."

"Be very nice," said Mr. Sloane, without gratitude. "Well—I think we ought to be starting home."

"Please don't rush off," Gatsby pleaded with them. He had regained his composure now, and he was eager to spend more time with Tom. "Why don't you—why don't you stay for dinner? I wouldn't be surprised if some other people showed up from New York."

"You're coming to dinner with me," the lady said enthusiastically. "Both of you."

This included me. Mr. Sloane stood up.

"Come along," he said—but to her only.

"I'm serious," she insisted. "I'd really like you to stay. There's plenty of space."

Gatsby looked at me with a questioning expression. He wanted to go and he couldn't see that Mr. Sloane had decided he shouldn't.

"I'm afraid I won't be able to," I said.

"Well, you come," she urged, focusing on Gatsby.

Mr. Sloane whispered something close to her ear.

"We won't be late if we start now," she insisted aloud.

"I don't have a horse," Gatsby said. "I used to ride when I was in the army, but I've never owned a horse. I'll need to follow you in my car. Give me just a moment."

The rest of us stepped out onto the porch, where Sloane and the woman started having an intense private conversation.

"My God, I think the man is actually coming," Tom said. "Doesn't he realize she doesn't want him?"

"She says she does want him."

"She's throwing a big dinner party and he won't know anyone there." He frowned. "I wonder where the hell he met Daisy. I swear, I might be old-fashioned in my thinking, but women get around way too much these days for my liking. They meet all sorts of crazy people."

Suddenly Mr. Sloane and the lady walked down the steps and got on their horses.

"Come on," Mr. Sloane said to Tom, "we're running late. We need to leave." Then he turned to me: "Let him know we couldn't wait around, okay?"

Tom and I shook hands, while the others and I exchanged brief, distant nods, and they hurried down the driveway, vanishing beneath the thick August leaves just as Gatsby emerged from the front door, carrying his hat and light coat.

Tom was clearly bothered by Daisy going around by herself, because the following Saturday night he came with her to Gatsby's party. Maybe his being there gave the evening its strange sense of heaviness—it stands out in my memory from Gatsby's other parties that summer. The same people were there, or at least the same type of people, the same abundance of champagne, the same colorful, chaotic excitement, but I sensed something unpleasant in the atmosphere, a spreading roughness that hadn't existed before. Or maybe I had simply gotten used to it, learned to accept West Egg as a complete world unto itself, with its own standards and its own important figures, inferior to nothing because it had no awareness of being so, and now I was seeing it again, through Daisy's eyes. It's always depressing to look through fresh eyes at things you've spent your own energy learning to accept.

They arrived at dusk, and as we walked out among the glittering crowds, Daisy's voice was making soft, murmuring sounds in her throat.

"These things thrill me so much," she whispered. "If you feel like kissing me at any point tonight, Nick, just tell me and I'll happily set it up for you. Simply say my name. Or show a green card. I'm handing out green—"

"Look around," suggested Gatsby.

"I'm looking around. I'm having a wonderful—"

"You must see the faces of many people you've heard about."

Tom's arrogant gaze swept across the crowd.

"We don't get out much," he said; "actually, I was just thinking that I don't know anyone here."

"Maybe you know that woman." Gatsby pointed to a stunning, almost otherworldly orchid of a woman who sat regally beneath a white-plum tree. Tom and Daisy gazed at her, experiencing that distinctly surreal sensation that comes with recognizing a previously phantom-like movie star in person.

"She's lovely," said Daisy.

"The man leaning over her is her director."

He formally escorted them from one group to another:

"Mrs. Buchanan... and Mr. Buchanan—" After a moment's hesitation he added: "the polo player."

"Oh no," Tom protested immediately, "not me."

But clearly the sound of it appealed to Gatsby because Tom stayed "the polo player" for the remainder of the evening.

"I've never encountered so many famous people," Daisy said with excitement. "I really enjoyed talking to that gentleman—what was his name again?—the one with that somewhat bluish nose."

Gatsby recognized him and mentioned that he was a small-time producer.

"Well, I liked him anyway."

"I'd prefer not to be the polo player," Tom said pleasantly. "I'd rather observe all these famous people in—in obscurity."

Daisy and Gatsby danced together. I recall feeling surprised by how gracefully and conservatively he performed the foxtrot—I had never witnessed him dancing before. Afterward, they strolled over to my house and settled on the front steps for thirty minutes, while I stayed in the garden keeping watch at her request. "Just in case there's a fire or a flood," she said, "or some other act of God."

Tom emerged from wherever he had been as we sat down for dinner together. "Would it be okay if I ate with some people over there?" he asked. "This guy is telling some really funny stories."

"Go ahead," Daisy replied warmly, "and if you need to write down any addresses, here's my little gold pencil."... After a moment, she glanced around and told me the girl was "ordinary but attractive," and I could tell that apart from the thirty minutes she had spent alone with Gatsby, she wasn't enjoying herself.

We were sitting at a table where everyone was especially drunk. That was my fault—Gatsby had been called away to take a phone call, and I had actually enjoyed being around these very same people just two weeks earlier. But what had entertained me back then now felt toxic and poisonous in the atmosphere.

"How do you feel, Miss Baedeker?"

The girl I was speaking to had been trying, without success, to lean against my shoulder. When I asked her this question, she straightened up and opened her eyes.

"Wha'?"

A large, sluggish woman who had been pressuring Daisy to play golf with her at the local club the next day spoke up in Miss Baedeker's defense:

"Oh, she's fine now. After she's had five or six cocktails, she always starts screaming like that. I keep telling her she should quit drinking."

"I do leave it alone," the accused stated in a hollow voice.

"We heard you shouting, so I told Doc Civet here: 'There's someone who needs your help, Doc.'"

"She's really grateful, I'm sure," said another friend without any appreciation, "but you soaked her entire dress when you shoved her head into the pool."

"The thing I hate most is getting my head stuck in a pool," mumbled Miss Baedeker. "They nearly drowned me once over in New Jersey."

"Then you should leave it alone," Doctor Civet replied.

"Speak for yourself!" Miss Baedeker shouted angrily. "Your hand is shaking. I wouldn't let you operate on me!"

It was exactly like that. One of the final things I can recall was standing beside Daisy and observing the film director and his leading actress. They remained beneath the white plum tree with their faces nearly touching, separated only by a slender, pale beam of moonlight. I realized that he had been gradually leaning closer to her throughout the entire evening to reach this intimate distance, and as I continued watching, I witnessed him bend that final inch and press a kiss to her cheek.

"I like her," said Daisy, "I think she's lovely."

But everything else bothered her—and undeniably because it wasn't just an act but a genuine feeling. She was horrified by West Egg, this unheard-of "place" that Broadway had created from a Long Island fishing village—horrified by its crude energy that bristled against the old polite pretenses and by the overly obvious destiny that drove its residents along a quick path from nowhere to nowhere. She found something terrible in the very straightforwardness that she couldn't comprehend.

I sat on the front steps with them while they waited for their car. It was dark out here in front; only the bright doorway cast about ten square feet of light into the gentle black morning. Occasionally a shadow shifted against a dressing-room window shade above, replaced by another shadow, creating an endless parade of silhouettes who applied rouge and powder before an unseen mirror.

"Who exactly is this Gatsby?" Tom demanded suddenly. "Some major bootlegger?"

"Where did you hear that?" I asked.

"I didn't hear it. I imagined it. A lot of these newly rich people are just big bootleggers, you know."

"Not Gatsby," I said curtly.

He stayed quiet for a moment. The small stones on the driveway made crunching sounds beneath his feet.

"Well, he definitely must have worked hard to put this collection of animals together."

A gentle wind ruffled the gray mist of Daisy's fur collar.

"At least they're more fascinating than the people we know," she said, forcing herself to speak.

"You didn't seem very interested."

"Well, I was."

Tom laughed and turned to me.

"Did you notice Daisy's face when that girl asked her to put her under a cold shower?"

Daisy started singing along with the music in a rough, rhythmic whisper, drawing out a significance from each word that it had never possessed before and would never possess again. As the melody climbed higher, her voice cracked beautifully, trailing along with it in the way that contralto voices do, and every shift released a bit of her warm human enchantment into the atmosphere.

"Many people show up without being invited," she said suddenly. "That girl wasn't invited. They just push their way in and he's too courteous to say anything."

"I want to know who he is and what he does," Tom insisted. "And I think I'll make it my business to find out."

"I can tell you right now," she replied. "He owned several pharmacies, quite a few of them actually. He built the business up from scratch."

The slow-moving limousine came rolling up the driveway.

"Good night, Nick," said Daisy.

Her gaze shifted away from me and moved toward the bright top of the stairs, where "Three O'Clock in the Morning," a simple, melancholy waltz popular that year, was floating through the open doorway. Despite everything, Gatsby's casual party held romantic possibilities that were completely missing from her own life. What was it in that music drifting down that seemed to be drawing her back inside? What might unfold during these mysterious, unpredictable hours ahead? Maybe some extraordinary guest would show up, someone incredibly rare and wonderful, perhaps a genuinely luminous young woman who, with just one fresh look at Gatsby, one instant of enchanted meeting, would erase those five years of constant dedication.

I remained there until late that evening. Gatsby had requested that I wait until he became available, so I remained in the garden until the expected group of swimmers had rushed up from the dark beach, cold and energized, and until the lights in the guest bedrooms above had been turned off. When he finally descended the stairs, his bronzed skin appeared unusually taut across his face, and his eyes looked both bright and weary.

"She didn't like it," he said immediately.

"Of course she did."

"She didn't like it," he insisted. "She didn't have a good time."

He remained quiet, and I could sense his overwhelming sadness that he couldn't put into words.

"I feel distant from her," he said. "It's difficult to get her to understand."

"You mean about the dance?"

"The dance?" He brushed off all the dances he had hosted with a quick snap of his fingers. "Old sport, the dance doesn't matter."

He wanted nothing less from Daisy than for her to go to Tom and tell him: "I never loved you." Once she had erased those four years with that single statement, they could figure out the more practical steps they needed to take. One of those steps was that, after she was free, they would return to Louisville and get married from her house—exactly as if it were five years earlier.

"And she doesn't understand," he said. "She used to be able to understand. We'd sit for hours—"

He stopped speaking and started walking back and forth along a barren pathway littered with fruit peels, thrown-away party favors, and trampled flowers.

"I wouldn't ask too much of her," I suggested. "You can't repeat the past."

"Can't repeat the past?" he cried in disbelief. "Why of course you can!"

He looked around frantically, as though the past was hiding there in the shadows of his house, just beyond his grasp.

"I'm going to fix everything just the way it was before," he said, nodding determinedly. "She'll see."

He spoke extensively about the past, and I understood that he was trying to reclaim something—perhaps some sense of who he was—that had been lost when he fell in love with Daisy. His life had been chaotic and unsettled ever since, but if he could somehow go back to that particular moment and carefully retrace his steps, he might be able to discover what that missing piece was...

One autumn night, five years earlier, they had been walking down the street as leaves fell around them, and they reached a spot where no trees grew and the sidewalk gleamed white in the moonlight. They paused there and faced each other. The evening was cool and filled with that enigmatic thrill that arrives during the two seasonal transitions of the year. The soft lights from the houses glowed outward into the night and there was movement and activity among the stars. From the edge of his vision Gatsby noticed that the sections of the sidewalk actually formed a stairway that rose to a hidden place above the trees—he could ascend to it, if he climbed by himself, and once he arrived there he could drink from life's nourishment, swallow the extraordinary essence of amazement.

His heart pounded as Daisy's pale face drew close to his. He understood that once he kissed this girl and bound his indescribable dreams to her mortal breath forever, his mind would never again wander freely like God's mind. So he hesitated, listening a moment longer to the tuning fork that had been struck against a star. Then he kissed her. When his lips touched hers, she bloomed for him like a flower, and the transformation was complete.

Throughout everything he spoke, even amid his terrible sentimentality, something stirred in my memory—a fleeting rhythm, a piece of forgotten words that I had encountered somewhere long ago. For an instant, a phrase attempted to form on my tongue and my lips opened like those of a mute person, as if something more substantial than a breath of surprised air was fighting to emerge from them. Yet they produced no sound, and whatever I had nearly recalled remained forever beyond expression.

Part 7

It was when curiosity about Gatsby reached its peak that the lights in his house failed to turn on one Saturday night—and, as mysteriously as it had started, his role as Trimalchio came to an end. Only slowly did I realize that the cars which turned hopefully into his driveway stayed for just a moment and then drove away in disappointment. Wondering if he might be ill I walked over to investigate—an unknown butler with a menacing face peered at me with suspicion from the doorway.

"Is Mr. Gatsby sick?"

"No." After a moment he reluctantly added "sir" in a slow, resentful manner.

"I hadn't seen him around, and I was quite concerned. Tell him Mr. Carraway stopped by."

"Who?" he asked rudely.

"Carraway."

"Carraway. All right, I'll tell him."

Suddenly he slammed the door shut.

My Finnish friend told me that Gatsby had fired all the servants in his house a week earlier and brought in half a dozen new ones, who never ventured into West Egg village where the local merchants might bribe them, but instead ordered modest supplies by phone. The delivery boy from the grocery store said the kitchen was a complete mess, and most people in the village believed the new staff weren't really servants at all.

The next day, Gatsby called me on the phone.

"Are you leaving?" I asked.

"No, old sport."

"I hear you fired all your servants."

"I needed someone who wouldn't spread rumors. Daisy visits quite frequently—during the afternoons."

So the entire establishment had collapsed like a house of cards at the disapproval in her eyes.

"They're people that Wolfshiem wanted to help out. They're all family - brothers and sisters. They used to operate a small hotel."

"I see."

He was calling at Daisy's request—would I come to lunch at her house tomorrow? Miss Baker would be there. Half an hour later Daisy herself called and seemed relieved to discover that I was coming. Something was going on. And yet I couldn't believe that they would pick this moment for a confrontation—especially for the rather distressing scene that Gatsby had described in the garden.

The following day was scorching hot, nearly the final day of summer and definitely the hottest one yet. When my train came out of the tunnel into the bright sunlight, only the blazing whistles from the National Biscuit Company pierced through the sweltering silence of midday. The wicker seats in the train car seemed ready to burst into flames; the woman sitting beside me sweated gently for a time into her white blouse, and then, as her newspaper grew damp beneath her touch, she gave up completely to the intense heat with a hopeless moan. Her purse dropped to the floor.

"Oh, my!" she gasped.

I picked it up with a tired stoop and gave it back to her, keeping it at arm's length and gripping only the very edges to show that I had no intentions toward it—but everyone nearby, including the woman, still suspected me anyway.

"Hot!" the conductor called out to the familiar faces around him. "What weather we're having!... Hot!... Hot!... Hot!... Is it hot enough for you? Is it hot? Is it...?"

My train ticket was returned to me with a dark smudge from his hand. In this sweltering heat, who could possibly care whose flushed lips he had kissed, or whose head had dampened the pajama pocket over his heart!

Through the hallway of the Buchanans' house, a gentle breeze carried the sound of the ringing telephone to where Gatsby and I stood waiting at the door.

"The master's body?" the butler shouted into the phone. "I'm sorry, ma'am, but we can't provide it—it's way too hot to handle right now!"

"What he really said was: "Yes... Yes... I'll see.""

He hung up the phone and walked toward us, with a slight sheen on his skin, to collect our rigid straw hats.

"Madame is waiting for you in the salon!" he shouted, pointing unnecessarily toward the room. In this sweltering heat, every unnecessary movement felt like an assault on everyone's shared energy.

The room was dark and cool, well-shaded by awnings. Daisy and Jordan reclined on a massive couch, resembling silver statues as their white dresses pressed down against the humming breeze from the fans.

"We can't move," they said together.

Jordan's fingers, dusted with white powder over their tanned skin, lingered briefly in mine.

"And Mr. Thomas Buchanan, the athlete?" I asked.

At the same time, I heard his voice on the hallway phone—rough, muted, and raspy.

Gatsby stood in the center of the red carpet and looked around with captivated eyes. Daisy observed him and laughed, her sweet, thrilling laugh; a small cloud of powder drifted from her chest into the air.

"Word is," Jordan whispered, "that's Tom's girlfriend on the phone."

We stayed quiet. The voice in the hallway grew louder with irritation: "Fine then, I'm not going to sell you the car at all... I don't owe you anything... and I won't tolerate you pestering me about this during lunch!"

"Holding down the receiver," Daisy said cynically.

"No, he's not," I assured her. "It's a legitimate deal. I happen to know about it."

Tom threw the door wide open, filling the entire doorway for a moment with his heavy frame, and rushed into the room.

"Mr. Gatsby!" He extended his broad, flat hand with carefully hidden dislike. "I'm pleased to see you, sir… Nick…"

"Make us a cold drink," cried Daisy.

As he walked out of the room again, she stood up and moved over to Gatsby, pulling his face down toward hers and kissing him on the lips.

"You know I love you," she whispered softly.

"You forget there's a lady present," said Jordan.

Daisy glanced around uncertainly.

"You kiss Nick too."

"What a low, vulgar girl!"

"I don't care!" Daisy shouted, and started dancing heavily on the brick fireplace. Then she remembered how hot it was and sat down on the couch with a guilty expression just as a nurse in clean, fresh clothes walked into the room leading a little girl.

"Blessed precious," she cooed softly, extending her arms toward him. "Come to your own mother who loves you."

The child, released by the nurse, hurried across the room and nestled shyly against her mother's dress.

"The blessed precious! Did mother get powder on your old yellow hair? Stand up now, and say—How do you do."

Gatsby and I both leaned down and grasped the small, hesitant hand. After that, he continued staring at the child with amazement. I don't believe he had ever truly accepted that the child was real until that moment.

"I got dressed before lunch," said the child, turning eagerly to Daisy.

"That's because your mother wanted to show you off." Her face tilted down, creating a single crease in her small white neck. "You're such a dreamer. You absolute little dreamer."

"Yes," the child admitted calmly. "Aunt Jordan is wearing a white dress too."

"How do you like mother's friends?" Daisy turned her around so that she faced Gatsby. "Do you think they're pretty?"

"Where's Daddy?"

"She doesn't look like her father," Daisy explained. "She looks like me. She has my hair and the shape of my face."

Daisy leaned back against the couch. The nurse moved forward and extended her hand.

"Come, Pammy."

"Goodbye, sweetheart!"

With a hesitant look back, the well-behaved child gripped her nurse's hand and was led through the doorway, just as Tom returned, walking ahead of four gin rickeys that clinked with ice.

Gatsby picked up his drink.

"They definitely look cool," he said, with obvious tension.

We drank in long, eager gulps.

"I read somewhere that the sun's getting hotter every year," Tom said cheerfully. "It looks like pretty soon the earth's going to fall into the sun—or hold on—it's actually the opposite—the sun's getting colder every year."

"Come outside," he suggested to Gatsby, "I'd like you to have a look at the place."

I walked with them out to the veranda. On the green Sound, still and motionless in the heat, a single small sail moved slowly toward the cooler open water. Gatsby's eyes tracked it briefly; he lifted his hand and gestured across the bay.

"I'm right across from you."

"So you are."

Our eyes rose above the rose gardens and the scorching lawn and the overgrown debris of late summer along the shoreline. Gradually the white sails of the boat drifted against the blue cool edge of the sky. Before us stretched the rippling ocean and the abundant blessed islands.

"That's entertainment for you," said Tom, nodding. "I'd like to be out there with him for about an hour."

We had lunch in the dining room, which was also darkened to keep out the heat, and we drank cold beer while forcing ourselves to be cheerful despite our nervousness.

"What are we going to do with ourselves this afternoon?" cried Daisy, "and the day after that, and the next thirty years?"

"Don't be morbid," Jordan said. "Life starts all over again when it gets crisp in the fall."

"But it's so hot," Daisy insisted, nearly in tears, "and everything's so mixed up. Let's all go into town!"

Her voice fought its way through the oppressive heat, pushing against it and shaping its meaningless intensity into recognizable forms.

"I've heard of turning a stable into a garage," Tom was telling Gatsby, "but I'm the first person who ever turned a garage into a stable."

"Who wants to go to town?" Daisy asked insistently. Gatsby's eyes drifted toward her. "Ah," she exclaimed, "you look so cool."

Their eyes met, and they gazed at each other, alone in their own world. With some effort, she looked down at the table.

"You always look so cool," she said again.

She had told him that she loved him, and Tom Buchanan witnessed it. He was shocked. His mouth fell open slightly, and he stared at Gatsby, then turned back to look at Daisy as though he was seeing her for the first time in years, like someone from his

116

distant past.

"You look just like the man in the advertisement," she continued innocently. "You know the advertisement with the man—"

"All right," Tom interrupted quickly, "I'm perfectly willing to go to town. Come on—we're all going to town."

He stood up, his gaze still darting back and forth between Gatsby and his wife. Nobody moved.

"Come on!" His patience snapped slightly. "What's wrong, anyway? If we're heading to town, let's get going."

His hand shook as he struggled to control himself, bringing the last of his beer to his lips. Daisy's voice made us stand up and walk out onto the scorching gravel driveway.

"Are we just going to leave?" she protested. "Just like that? Aren't we going to let anyone have a cigarette first?"

"Everyone smoked throughout the entire lunch."

"Oh, let's have some fun," she pleaded with him. "It's way too hot to worry about anything."

He didn't answer.

"Have it your own way," she said. "Come on, Jordan."

They headed upstairs to prepare while the three of us men remained below, kicking at the heated stones beneath our feet. A crescent moon already hung suspended in the western sky. Gatsby began to say something, then thought better of it, but not before Tom had turned around and looked at him with anticipation.

"Do you keep your stables here?" Gatsby asked, struggling to make conversation.

"About a quarter of a mile down the road."

"Oh."

A pause.

"I don't understand why we need to go into town," Tom burst out angrily. "Women get these ideas in their heads—"

"Should we bring something to drink?" Daisy called out from an upstairs window.

"I'll get some whisky," Tom replied. He walked inside.

Gatsby turned to me stiffly:

"I can't say anything in his house, old sport."

"She has an indiscreet voice," I observed. "It's full of—" I paused.

"Her voice is full of money," he said suddenly.

That was it. I had never understood it before. Her voice was full of money—that was the endless charm that rose and fell within it, the jingling sound of it, the musical ring of it like cymbals... High up in a white palace lived the king's daughter, the golden girl...

Tom emerged from the house, wrapping a quart bottle in a towel, with Daisy and Jordan following behind him wearing small, fitted hats made of metallic fabric and carrying lightweight capes draped over their arms.

"Should we all take my car?" Gatsby suggested. He touched the hot, green leather of the seat. "I should have parked it in the shade."

"Is it standard shift?" Tom asked.

"Yes."

"Well, you take my coupe and let me drive your car to town."

The suggestion was distasteful to Gatsby.

"I don't think there's much gas," he objected.

"We have plenty of gas," Tom said loudly and energetically. He glanced at the fuel gauge. "And if we run out, I can pull over at a pharmacy. You can buy just about anything at a pharmacy these days."

A pause followed this seemingly meaningless comment. Daisy glanced at Tom with a frown, and an indescribable expression crossed Gatsby's face—one that was both completely unfamiliar and somehow vaguely recognizable, as though I had only heard it described in words before.

"Come on, Daisy," said Tom, pressing her with his hand toward Gatsby's car. "I'll take you in this circus wagon."

He opened the door, but she stepped away from his embrace.

"You take Nick and Jordan. We'll follow you in the coupé."

She moved close to Gatsby, her hand brushing against his coat. Jordan, Tom, and I climbed into the front seat of Gatsby's car, and Tom cautiously worked the unfamiliar gears before we sped away into the stifling heat, leaving the two of them behind and out of view.

"Did you see that?" Tom asked.

"See what?"

He stared at me intently, understanding that Jordan and I must have been aware the entire time.

"You think I'm pretty stupid, don't you?" he said. "Maybe I am, but I have this—almost like a sixth sense, sometimes, that shows me what I need to do. You probably don't believe that, but science—"

He stopped. The urgent situation at hand caught up with him, drawing him back from the brink of abstract speculation.

"I've done a little research on this guy," he went on. "I could have dug deeper if I'd known—"

"Are you saying you've visited a psychic?" Jordan asked with amusement.

"What?" Confused, he stared at us as we laughed. "A medium?"

"About Gatsby."

"About Gatsby! No, I haven't. I said I'd been doing a little research into his background."

"And you discovered he was an Oxford man," said Jordan helpfully.

"An Oxford man!" He couldn't believe it. "No way in hell! He's wearing a pink suit."

"Nevertheless he's an Oxford man."

"Oxford, New Mexico," Tom scoffed dismissively, "or something like that."

"Listen, Tom. If you're such a snob, why did you invite him to lunch?" Jordan asked irritably.

"Daisy invited him; she knew him before we got married—God knows where!"

We were all feeling irritable as the effects of the alcohol wore off, and recognizing this, we drove in silence for some time. When Doctor T. J. Eckleburg's faded eyes appeared in the distance down the road, I recalled Gatsby's warning about the gasoline.

"We have enough to get us to town," said Tom.

"But there's a garage right here," Jordan protested. "I don't want to break down in this scorching heat."

Tom slammed on both brakes with frustration, and we skidded to a sudden, dust-filled halt beneath Wilson's sign. A moment later, the owner appeared from inside his business and stared at the car with hollow, empty eyes.

"Let's get some gas!" Tom said harshly. "What do you think we stopped for—to admire the view?"

"I'm sick," Wilson said without moving. "I've been sick all day."

"What's the matter?"

"I'm completely exhausted."

"Well, should I take care of this myself?" Tom asked. "You seemed fine when we talked on the phone."

With considerable effort, Wilson stepped away from the shade and support of the doorway and, breathing heavily, unscrewed the cap of the tank. In the bright sunlight, his face appeared green.

"I didn't mean to interrupt your lunch," he said. "But I really need money, and I was wondering what you planned to do with your old car."

"What do you think of this one?" Tom asked. "I picked it up last week."

"It's a nice yellow one," said Wilson, as he pulled hard on the handle.

"Would you like to buy it?"

"Fat chance," Wilson smiled weakly. "No, but I could make some money on the other."

"What do you suddenly need money for?"

"I've been here too long. I want to get away. My wife and I want to go West."

"Your wife does," Tom burst out, clearly shocked.

"She's been talking about it for ten years." He paused for a moment against the pump, shielding his eyes from the light. "And now she's leaving whether she wants to or not. I'm going to take her away."

The car sped past us in a cloud of dust with the quick glimpse of someone waving.

"What do I owe you?" Tom asked harshly.

"I just figured out something strange over the past couple of days," Wilson said. "That's why I want to leave. That's why I've been pestering you about the car."

"What do I owe you?"

"One dollar and twenty cents."

The intense, pounding heat was starting to make me feel disoriented, and I experienced a moment of panic before I understood that his doubts hadn't yet focused on Tom. He had found out that Myrtle had been living some kind of separate existence away from him in a different world, and the revelation had left him physically ill. I looked at him and then at Tom, who had made a similar realization less than an hour earlier—and it struck me that there was no distinction between men, whether in intellect or background, as deep as the distinction between those who are sick and those who are healthy. Wilson was so unwell that he appeared guilty, inexcusably guilty—as though he had just gotten some innocent girl pregnant.

"I'll let you have that car," Tom said. "I'll send it over tomorrow afternoon."

That place had always made me feel uneasy, even in the bright afternoon sunlight, and now I turned my head as if something behind me had caught my attention. Above the ash-heaps, the enormous eyes of Doctor T. J. Eckleburg continued their watch, but I noticed, after a moment, that other eyes were looking at us with unusual intensity from less than twenty feet away.

In one of the windows above the garage, the curtains had been pulled back slightly, and Myrtle Wilson was looking down at the car. She was so absorbed that she didn't realize anyone was watching her, and different emotions appeared on her face one after another like images slowly forming in a photograph. Her expression was strangely familiar—it was a look I had frequently seen on women's faces, but on Myrtle Wilson's face it appeared meaningless and puzzling until I understood that her eyes, wide with jealous fear, were focused not on Tom, but on Jordan Baker, whom she believed to be his wife.

There is no confusion like the confusion of a simple mind, and as we drove away Tom was feeling the sharp stings of panic. His wife and his mistress, until an hour ago safe and untouchable, were rapidly slipping from his control. Instinct made him press down on the gas pedal with the dual purpose of catching up to Daisy and leaving Wilson behind, and we raced toward Astoria at fifty miles an hour, until, among the web-like steel beams of the elevated railway, we spotted the leisurely blue coupé.

"Those big movie theaters around Fiftieth Street are great," Jordan suggested. "I love New York on summer afternoons when everyone's gone. There's something very sensual about it— overripe, as if all kinds of strange fruits were about to fall right into your hands."

The word "sensuous" made Tom even more uncomfortable, but before he could come up with an objection, the coupé stopped, and Daisy motioned for us to pull up next to them.

"Where are we going?" she cried.

"How about the movies?"

"It's so hot," she complained. "You go ahead. We'll drive around and meet up with you later." She managed to summon a bit of her usual humor. "We'll find you on some street corner. I'll be the woman smoking two cigarettes."

"We can't discuss this here," Tom said with frustration, as a truck blared its horn angrily behind us. "Follow me to the south side of Central Park, in front of the Plaza."

Several times he turned his head and looked back for their car, and whenever traffic delayed them he slowed down until they came into view. I think he was worried they would suddenly turn down a side street and disappear from his life forever.

But they didn't. And we all took the less understandable step of booking the living room of a suite at the Plaza Hotel.

The long and chaotic argument that ultimately led us to that room escapes my memory, although I clearly recall the physical sensation of my underwear continuously creeping up my legs like a wet snake and occasional drops of sweat running cold down my back. The idea started when Daisy suggested we rent five bathrooms to take cold baths, and then it evolved into something more concrete as "a place to have a mint julep." We each kept repeating that it was a "crazy idea"—we all spoke simultaneously to a confused clerk and believed, or acted like we believed, that we were being very amusing…

The room was spacious and suffocating, and even though it was already four o'clock, opening the windows only let in a wave of hot air from the shrubs in the Park. Daisy walked over to the mirror and turned her back to us, adjusting her hair.

"It's a fantastic suite," Jordan whispered with respect, and everyone laughed.

"Open another window," Daisy ordered, without turning around.

"There aren't any more."

"Well, we'd better call for an axe—"

"The thing to do is to forget about the heat," Tom said irritably. "You make it ten times worse by complaining about it."

He unwrapped the whisky bottle from the towel and placed it on the table.

"Why don't you just leave her alone, old sport?" Gatsby said. "You're the one who wanted to come into the city."

There was a moment of silence. The telephone book slipped from its nail and splashed to the floor, and Jordan whispered, "Excuse me"—but this time no one laughed.

"I'll pick it up," I offered.

"I've got it." Gatsby looked at the separated string, murmured "Hum!" with interest, and threw the book onto a chair.

"That's a great expression of yours, isn't it?" Tom said sharply.

"What is?"

"All this 'old sport' business. Where'd you pick that up?"

"Listen, Tom," Daisy said, spinning away from the mirror, "if you're going to start making personal comments, I'm not staying here another second. Pick up the phone and order some ice for the mint juleps."

As Tom picked up the phone, the stifling heat suddenly burst into sound, and we found ourselves listening to the dramatic chords of Mendelssohn's Wedding March drifting up from the ballroom downstairs.

"Imagine getting married in this heat!" Jordan exclaimed miserably.

"Still—I got married in the middle of June," Daisy recalled. "Louisville in June! Someone fainted. Who was it that fainted,

Tom?"

"Biloxi," he replied curtly.

"A man named Biloxi. 'Blocks' Biloxi, and he made boxes—
that's a fact—and he was from Biloxi, Tennessee."

"They brought him to our house," Jordan continued, "since
we lived only two doors down from the church. He ended up
staying for three weeks, until my father told him he needed to leave.
The day after he left, my father passed away." She paused for a
moment, then added as though she worried she might have
seemed disrespectful, "There wasn't any connection between the
two things."

"I used to know a Bill Biloxi from Memphis," I said.

"That was his cousin. I knew his entire family background
before he departed. He gave me an aluminum putter that I still use
today."

The music had faded as the ceremony started, and now a long
cheer drifted through the window, followed by scattered shouts of
"Yea—ea—ea!" and finally by an explosion of jazz as the dancing
commenced.

"We're getting old," said Daisy. "If we were young we'd get up
and dance."

"Remember Biloxi," Jordan warned her. "Where did you know
him, Tom?"

"Biloxi?" He focused hard, trying to remember. "I didn't know
him. He was a friend of Daisy's."

"He wasn't," she said firmly. "I had never seen him before. He
came down in the private car."

"Well, he said he knew you. He said he was raised in Louisville.
Asa Bird brought him around at the last minute and asked if we
had room for him."

Jordan smiled.

"He was probably hitchhiking his way home. He told me he
was president of your class at Yale."

Tom and I stared at each other with blank expressions. "Biloxi?"

"First of all, we didn't have any president—"

Gatsby's foot tapped out a brief, anxious rhythm and Tom suddenly looked at him.

"By the way, Mr. Gatsby, I understand you're an Oxford man."

"Not exactly."

"Oh, yes, I understand you went to Oxford."

"Yes—I went there."

A pause. Then Tom's voice, disbelieving and offensive:

"You must have gone there around the same time Biloxi went to New Haven."

Another pause. A waiter knocked and entered with crushed mint and ice, but the silence remained unbroken by his "thank you" and the gentle closing of the door. This enormous matter was finally going to be resolved.

"I told you I went there," said Gatsby.

"I heard you, but I'd like to know when."

"It was in 1919, I only stayed five months. That's why I can't really call myself an Oxford man."

Tom looked around to see if we shared his disbelief. But we were all looking at Gatsby.

"After the armistice ended, they offered this opportunity to some of the officers," he went on. "We were allowed to attend any university in England or France."

I felt the urge to stand up and give him a hearty pat on the back. I experienced one of those moments where my complete confidence in him was restored, something that had happened to me before.

Daisy stood up with a slight smile and walked over to the table.

"Open the whisky, Tom," she ordered, "and I'll make you a mint julep. Then you won't seem so stupid to yourself... Look at the mint!"

"Hold on," Tom said sharply, "I need to ask Mr. Gatsby one more question."

"Go on," Gatsby said politely.

"What kind of trouble are you trying to start in my house anyway?"

They were finally out in the open, and Gatsby felt satisfied.

"He isn't causing a scene," Daisy looked desperately from one to the other. "You're causing a scene. Please show a little self-control."

"Self-control!" Tom repeated in disbelief. "I guess the trendy thing now is to just sit back and let some random nobody make moves on your wife. Well, if that's what we're doing, you can count me out... These days people start by mocking family life and family values, and next thing you know they'll toss everything aside and allow marriages between black and white people."

Energized by his passionate rambling, he pictured himself standing alone on civilization's final frontier.

"We're all white here," Jordan whispered.

"I know I'm not very popular. I don't throw big parties. I suppose you have to turn your house into a complete mess if you want to have any friends in today's world."

Furious as I was, as all of us were, I found myself wanting to laugh every time he spoke. His transformation from a free-spirited rebel to a self-righteous moralist was so thorough.

"I have something to tell you, old sport—" Gatsby began. But Daisy sensed what he was planning to say.

"Please don't!" she interrupted helplessly. "Please let's all go home. Why don't we all go home?"

"That's a good idea," I said, standing up. "Come on, Tom. Nobody wants a drink."

"I want to know what Mr. Gatsby has to tell me."

"Your wife doesn't love you," said Gatsby. "She's never loved you. She loves me."

"You must be crazy!" Tom exclaimed without thinking.

Gatsby jumped up, his face bright with excitement.

"She never loved you, do you hear?" he shouted. "She only married you because I was poor and she was tired of waiting for me. It was a terrible mistake, but in her heart she never loved anyone except me!"

At this moment, Jordan and I attempted to leave, but Tom and Gatsby both insisted with stubborn determination that we stay— as if neither of them had anything to hide and it would be an honor for us to witness their emotional confrontation from the sidelines.

"Sit down, Daisy," Tom's voice struggled unsuccessfully to find a fatherly tone. "What's been happening? I want to hear everything about it."

"I told you what's been happening," said Gatsby. "It's been going on for five years—and you had no idea."

Tom turned sharply toward Daisy.

"You've been seeing this guy for five years?"

"Not seeing," Gatsby said. "No, we couldn't meet. But we both loved each other the entire time, old sport, and you had no idea. I used to laugh sometimes"—though there was no laughter in his eyes—"thinking that you didn't know."

"Oh—that's all." Tom tapped his thick fingers together like a clergyman and leaned back in his chair.

"You're insane!" he burst out. "I can't talk about what happened five years ago, because I didn't know Daisy back then— and I'll be damned if I understand how you got anywhere near her unless you were delivering groceries to the back door. But everything else you're saying is a complete lie. Daisy loved me when she married me and she loves me now."

"No," said Gatsby, shaking his head.

"She does, though. The problem is that sometimes she gets foolish ideas in her head and doesn't know what she's doing." He nodded wisely. "And what's more, I love Daisy too. Once in a while I go off on a wild time and make a fool of myself, but I always come back, and in my heart I love her all the time."

"You're disgusting," Daisy said. She turned toward me, and her voice dropped an octave lower, filling the room with electrifying contempt: "Do you know why we left Chicago? I'm surprised they didn't tell you the story of that little adventure."

Gatsby walked over and stood beside her.

"Daisy, that's all behind us now," he said with conviction. "None of it matters anymore. Just tell him the truth—that you never loved him—and everything will be erased forever."

She stared at him without really seeing. "Why—how could I possibly love him?"

"You never loved him."

She paused. Her gaze landed on Jordan and me with a kind of plea, as if she finally understood what she was doing—and as if she had never meant to do anything at all from the beginning. But it was finished now. It was too late.

"I never loved him," she said, with noticeable hesitation.

"Not at Kapiolani?" Tom asked suddenly.

"No."

From the ballroom below, muted and stifling musical notes floated upward on warm currents of air.

"Not that day I carried you down from the Punch Bowl to keep your shoes dry?" There was a husky tenderness in his tone… "Daisy?"

"Please don't." Her voice was cold, but the bitterness had disappeared from it. She looked at Gatsby. "There, Jay," she said—but her hand shook as she tried to light a cigarette. Suddenly she threw the cigarette and the burning match onto the carpet.

"Oh, you're asking for too much!" she cried out to Gatsby. "I love you right now—isn't that enough? I can't change what happened before." She started crying uncontrollably. "I did love him at one time—but I loved you as well."

Gatsby's eyes opened and closed.

"You loved me too?" he repeated.

"Even that's a lie," Tom said harshly. "She had no idea you were still alive. Listen—Daisy and I share things you'll never understand, experiences that neither of us will ever be able to forget."

The words appeared to cut into Gatsby like a physical blow.

"I need to talk to Daisy by myself," he demanded. "She's completely worked up right now—"

"Even alone I can't say I never loved Tom," she confessed in a heartbroken voice. "It wouldn't be honest."

"Of course it wouldn't," Tom agreed.

She turned to her husband.

"As if it mattered to you," she said.

"Of course it matters. I'm going to take better care of you from now on."

"You don't understand," Gatsby said, with a hint of panic in his voice. "You're not going to take care of her anymore."

"I'm not?" Tom's eyes widened as he laughed. He could afford to stay in control now. "Why is that?"

"Daisy's leaving you."

"Nonsense."

"I am, though," she said with obvious difficulty.

"She's not leaving me!" Tom's words suddenly loomed over Gatsby. "Certainly not for a common swindler who'd have to steal the ring he put on her finger."

"I won't stand this!" cried Daisy. "Oh, please let's get out."

"Who are you, anyway?" Tom burst out. "You're part of that group that associates with Meyer Wolfshiem—that much I know for certain. I've done some digging into your business—and I'll investigate further tomorrow."

"You can do whatever you want about that, old sport," said Gatsby calmly.

"I discovered what your 'drugstores' really were." He turned toward us and spoke quickly. "He and this Wolfshiem purchased numerous small drugstores on side streets here and in Chicago and sold grain alcohol directly to customers. That's one of his schemes. I suspected he was a bootlegger from the moment I first laid eyes on him, and I wasn't far off the mark."

"What about it?" Gatsby said politely. "I suppose your friend Walter Chase wasn't too proud to get involved in it."

"And you abandoned him when he needed you most, didn't you? You allowed him to spend a month in jail over in New Jersey. My God! You should hear what Walter has to say about you."

"He came to us completely broke. He was very happy to earn some money, old sport."

"Don't you call me 'old sport'!" Tom shouted. Gatsby remained silent. "Walter could have had you arrested under the gambling laws as well, but Wolfshiem frightened him into keeping quiet."

That strange but familiar expression had returned to Gatsby's face.

"That drugstore business was just small change," Tom continued slowly, "but you've got something going on now that Walter's afraid to tell me about."

I looked at Daisy, who was gazing in terror between Gatsby and her husband, and at Jordan, who had started balancing an invisible yet captivating object on the tip of her chin. Then I turned back to Gatsby—and was shocked by his expression. He appeared—and this is stated with complete disdain for the whispered gossip of his garden—as though he had "killed a man." For a moment his facial expression could be characterized in precisely that extraordinary way.

It passed, and he started talking frantically to Daisy, rejecting everything, protecting his reputation against charges that hadn't even been brought up. But with each word she withdrew deeper and deeper into herself, so he abandoned that approach, and only the lifeless dream continued fighting as the afternoon faded away, attempting to reach what could no longer be grasped, wrestling miserably, without hope, toward that vanished voice on the other side of the room.

The voice pleaded once more to leave.

"Please, Tom! I can't stand this anymore."

Her frightened eyes revealed that whatever intentions and courage she had possessed were completely gone.

"You two head home, Daisy," Tom said. "Take Mr. Gatsby's car."

She looked at Tom, now feeling alarmed, but he persisted with generous contempt.

"Go ahead. He won't bother you. I think he understands that his arrogant little flirtation has ended."

They disappeared without saying anything, suddenly cut off, turned into something random and alone, like spirits that we couldn't even feel sorry for anymore.

After a moment, Tom stood up and started wrapping the unopened bottle of whisky in the towel.

"Do you want any of this stuff? Jordan?... Nick?"

I didn't answer.

"Nick?" he asked again.

"What?"

"Want any?"

"No… I just remembered that today's my birthday."

I was thirty years old. Ahead of me lay the ominous, threatening path of a new decade.

It was seven o'clock when we climbed into the car with him and headed toward Long Island. Tom wouldn't stop talking, celebrating and laughing, but his voice felt as distant to Jordan and me as the foreign chatter from the sidewalk or the noise from the train tracks above. There are limits to how much we can care about other people's problems, and we were happy to let all their heartbreaking fights disappear along with the city lights behind us. Thirty—the prospect of ten years of being alone, fewer and fewer single men to meet, less and less passion for life, hair getting thinner. But Jordan was there next to me, and unlike Daisy, she was smart enough never to drag forgotten dreams from one stage of life to the next. As we crossed the dark bridge, her pale face gently rested against my coat's shoulder, and the frightening reality of turning thirty faded away with the comforting touch of her hand.

So we drove on toward death through the cooling twilight.

The young Greek man, Michaelis, who operated the coffee shop next to the ash-heaps, served as the main witness during the inquest. He had been sleeping through the oppressive heat until sometime after five o'clock, when he walked over to the garage and discovered George Wilson ill in his office—genuinely ill, as pale as his own light-colored hair and trembling throughout his entire body. Michaelis suggested that he should go to bed, but Wilson declined, explaining that he would lose a significant amount of business if he did so. While his neighbor was attempting to convince him otherwise, a loud commotion erupted from upstairs.

"I have my wife locked up there," Wilson explained calmly. "She's going to remain there until the day after tomorrow, and then we're going to move away."

Michaelis was shocked; they had lived next door to each other for four years, and Wilson had never appeared remotely capable of making such a declaration. Usually he was one of those exhausted men: when he wasn't at work, he would sit in a chair by the entrance and watch the people and vehicles that went by on the street. Whenever someone talked to him, he would always respond with a pleasant but bland laugh. He belonged to his wife rather than to himself.

So naturally Michaelis tried to discover what had taken place, but Wilson refused to speak—instead he started giving strange, distrustful looks to his visitor and questioning him about what he had been doing at specific times on particular days. Just as Michaelis was becoming uncomfortable, some workers walked past the door heading to his restaurant, and Michaelis seized the chance to leave, planning to return later. But he never did. He figured he simply forgot about it, that was all. When he stepped outside again, shortly after seven o'clock, the conversation came back to him because he could hear Mrs. Wilson's voice, loud and harsh, coming from downstairs in the garage.

"Beat me!" he heard her cry. "Throw me down and beat me, you dirty little coward!"

A moment later she rushed out into the dusk, waving her hands and shouting—before he could move from his door the business was over.

The "death car," as the newspapers labeled it, didn't stop; it emerged from the approaching darkness, swerved tragically for a moment, and then vanished around the next curve. Mavro Michaelis wasn't even certain of its color—he told the first police officer that it was light green. The other vehicle, the one heading toward New York, came to a halt a hundred yards further on, and its driver rushed back to where Myrtle Wilson, her life brutally snuffed out, lay crumpled in the road as her thick dark blood mixed with the dust.

Michaelis and the other man got to her before anyone else, but after they tore open her blouse, which was still wet with sweat, they could see that her left breast hung loosely like a piece of torn fabric, and there was no point in checking for a heartbeat underneath. Her mouth gaped open and was slightly torn at the edges, as if she had struggled briefly while releasing the enormous life force she had kept within herself for so long.

We spotted the three or four cars and the crowd while we were still quite far away.

"Wreck!" Tom exclaimed. "That's excellent. Wilson will finally have some work to do."

He reduced his speed, though he had no plans to stop, until we drew closer and the quiet, focused expressions on the faces of the people gathered at the garage entrance caused him to instinctively apply the brakes.

"We'll take a look," he said doubtfully, "just a look."

I now noticed a hollow, wailing sound that came continuously from the garage, a sound that became clearer as we stepped out of the car and walked toward the door, revealing itself to be the words "Oh, my God!" repeated over and over in a gasping moan.

"There's some serious trouble here," said Tom excitedly.

He stretched up on his tiptoes and looked over the circle of heads surrounding him to see into the garage, which was illuminated only by a yellow light hanging in a swinging metal fixture above. Then he made a rough noise in his throat, and using a forceful pushing motion with his strong arms, he shoved his way through the crowd.

The circle formed again with people murmuring their protests as they moved; it took a moment before I could see anything clearly. Then newcomers disrupted the formation, and Jordan and I found ourselves suddenly pushed into the center.

Myrtle Wilson's body lay on a worktable against the wall, wrapped in a blanket and then covered with another blanket, as if she were cold on this sweltering night. Tom stood with his back to us, leaning over her motionless form. Beside him, a motorcycle officer was sweating profusely as he wrote down names in a small notebook, making frequent corrections. At first, I couldn't locate where the high-pitched, agonized sounds that rang loudly through the empty garage were coming from—then I spotted Wilson standing in the elevated doorway of his office, rocking back and forth while gripping the door frame with both hands. A man was speaking to him quietly and occasionally trying to place a comforting hand on his shoulder, but Wilson didn't hear or notice him. His gaze would slowly drift down from the overhead light to the covered table against the wall, then snap back up to the light, while he continuously let out his piercing, terrible cry:

"Oh, my God! Oh, my God! Oh, God! Oh, my God!"

Soon Tom suddenly raised his head and, after looking around the garage with unfocused eyes, made a confused, unclear comment to the police officer.

"M-a-v—" the police officer was saying, "—o—"

"No, r—" the man corrected, "M-a-v-r-o—"

"Listen to me!" Tom muttered fiercely.

"r—" said the policeman, "o—"

"g—"

"g—" He glanced up as Tom's large hand came down hard on his shoulder. "What do you want, buddy?"

"What happened?—that's what I want to know."

"A car hit her. She was killed instantly."

"Killed instantly," Tom repeated, staring.

"She ran out into the road. The son-of-a-bitch didn't even stop his car."

"There were two cars," said Michaelis, "one coming, one going, see?"

"Where are you going?" the policeman asked sharply.

"One train going each direction. Well, she"—his hand moved toward the blankets but stopped halfway and dropped to his side—"she ran out there and the one coming from New York hit her head-on, traveling thirty or forty miles per hour."

"What's the name of this place?" the officer demanded.

"Doesn't have a name."

A pale, well-dressed Black man stepped closer.

"It was a yellow car," he said, "big yellow car. New."

"Did you see the accident?" the police officer asked.

"No, but the car passed me down the road, going faster than forty. Going fifty, sixty."

"Come here and tell me your name. Watch out now. I want to find out what his name is."

Some words from this conversation must have reached Wilson, who was swaying in the office doorway, because suddenly a new theme emerged among his desperate cries:

"You don't have to tell me what kind of car it was! I know what kind of car it was!"

Watching Tom, I noticed the thick muscles behind his shoulder tensing beneath his jacket. He strode quickly toward Wilson and positioned himself directly in front of him, gripping him tightly by the upper arms.

"You need to get yourself together," he said with gentle roughness.

Wilson's eyes landed on Tom; he rose up on his tiptoes and then would have crumpled to his knees if Tom hadn't kept him standing.

"Listen," said Tom, giving him a slight shake. "I just arrived a minute ago from New York. I was bringing you that coupe we've been discussing. That yellow car I was driving this afternoon wasn't mine—do you understand? I haven't seen it all afternoon."

Only the Black man and I were close enough to hear what he said, but the police officer picked up on something in his tone and glanced over with hostile eyes.

"What's all that?" he demanded.

"I'm a friend of his." Tom turned his head but kept his hands steady on Wilson's body. "He says he knows the car that did it... It was a yellow car."

Some vague instinct prompted the police officer to eye Tom with suspicion.

"And what color is your car?"

"It's a blue car, a coupé."

"We just came directly from New York," I said.

Someone who had been driving a short distance behind us confirmed this, and the police officer turned away.

"Now, if you could give me that name again correctly—"

Picking up Wilson as if he were a doll, Tom carried him into the office, placed him in a chair, and returned.

"If someone will come here and stay with him," he said sharply with authority. He observed as the two men standing nearest looked at each other and reluctantly entered the room. Then Tom closed the door behind them and stepped down the single step, keeping his eyes away from the table. As he walked close by me he whispered: "Let's get out of here."

Self-consciously, with his commanding arms clearing the path, we forced our way through the crowd that was still forming, walking past a rushed doctor carrying his medical bag, who had been summoned in desperate hope thirty minutes earlier.

Tom drove slowly until we passed the curve—then he pressed the accelerator hard, and the car sped through the darkness. Soon I heard a quiet, rough sob, and noticed that tears were streaming down his face.

"The damn coward!" he whimpered. "He didn't even stop his car."

The Buchanan house suddenly appeared before us through the dark, whispering trees. Tom came to a halt next to the porch and gazed up at the second floor, where two windows glowed brightly amid the climbing vines.

"Daisy's home," he said. As we stepped out of the car, he looked at me and frowned a little.

"I should have dropped you off in West Egg, Nick. There's nothing we can do tonight."

A transformation had taken place in him, and he now spoke with seriousness and determination. As we walked across the moonlit gravel toward the porch, he handled the situation with a few quick, decisive words.

"I'll call for a taxi to take you home, and while you're waiting, you and Jordan should go to the kitchen and have them prepare some dinner for you—if you'd like." He opened the door. "Come in."

"No, thanks. But I'd appreciate it if you could call me a taxi. I'll wait outside."

Jordan placed her hand on my arm.

"Won't you come in, Nick?"

"No, thanks."

I was feeling slightly unwell and wanted some solitude. However, Jordan stayed a bit longer.

"It's only half-past nine," she said.

I'd be damned if I was going inside; I'd had my fill of everyone for one day, and suddenly that feeling extended to Jordan as well. She must have noticed something in my face, because she turned sharply away and hurried up the porch steps into the house. I sat there for a few minutes with my head buried in my hands, until I heard someone pick up the phone inside and the butler's voice requesting a taxi. Then I walked slowly down the driveway away from the house, planning to wait by the gate.

I hadn't walked twenty yards when I heard someone call my name and Gatsby emerged from between two bushes onto the path. I must have been feeling pretty strange by then, because all I could focus on was how his pink suit glowed in the moonlight.

"What are you doing?" I asked.

"Just standing here, old sport."

Somehow, that struck me as a contemptible way to make a living. For all I could tell, he might be planning to burglarize the house at any moment; it wouldn't have shocked me to spot menacing faces, the faces of "Wolfshiem's people," lurking behind him in the shadowy bushes.

"Did you see any trouble on the road?" he asked after a minute.

"Yes."

He hesitated.

"Was she killed?"

"Yes."

"I thought so; I told Daisy I thought so. It's better that the shock should all come at once. She stood it pretty well."

He spoke as though Daisy's response was the only thing that mattered.

"I reached West Egg using a back road," he continued, "and parked the car in my garage. I don't believe anyone spotted us, but naturally I can't be certain."

I had grown to dislike him so intensely by that point that I saw no need to inform him of his mistake.

"Who was the woman?" he asked.

"Her name was Wilson. Her husband owns the garage. How the devil did it happen?"

"Well, I tried to turn the wheel—" He stopped mid-sentence, and suddenly I realized what had really happened.

"Was Daisy driving?"

"Yes," he said after a moment, "but naturally I'll claim I was driving. You have to understand, when we departed from New York she was extremely anxious and she believed it would calm her nerves to take the wheel—and this woman suddenly ran out toward us just as we were overtaking a car traveling in the opposite direction. Everything occurred within seconds, but it appeared to me that she was trying to get our attention, assuming we were people she recognized. Well, initially Daisy swerved away from the woman toward the oncoming car, and then she panicked and jerked back. The instant my hand touched the steering wheel I felt the impact—it must have killed her immediately."

"It tore her apart—"

"Don't tell me, old sport." He winced. "Anyway—Daisy stepped on it. I tried to get her to stop, but she couldn't, so I pulled the emergency brake. Then she collapsed into my lap and I kept driving.

"She'll be fine tomorrow," he said after a moment. "I'm just going to stay here and watch to see if he tries to hassle her about that trouble this afternoon. She's locked herself in her room, and if he tries anything violent, she's going to flash the light on and off."

"He won't touch her," I said. "He's not thinking about her."

"I don't trust him, old sport."

"How long are you going to wait?"

"All night, if necessary. Anyway, until they all go to bed."

A fresh perspective suddenly struck me. What if Tom discovered that Daisy had been behind the wheel? He could perceive some kind of link in that revelation—his mind might jump to any number of conclusions. I gazed toward the house; several bright windows glowed downstairs, along with the soft pink light emanating from Daisy's room on the first floor.

"You stay here," I said. "I'll check if there's any indication of trouble."

I walked back along the edge of the lawn, crossed the gravel quietly, and crept up the veranda steps on my toes. The living room curtains were open, and I could see the room was empty. Moving across the porch where we had eaten dinner that June evening three months earlier, I reached a small square of light that I assumed was the pantry window. The shade was pulled down, but I discovered a gap at the bottom.

Daisy and Tom sat across from each other at the kitchen table, with a plate of cold fried chicken placed between them and two bottles of beer. He spoke to her with intense focus across the table, and his earnestness had caused his hand to rest upon and cover hers. Occasionally she would glance up at him and nod in agreement.

They weren't happy, and neither of them had touched the chicken or the beer—yet they weren't unhappy either. There was an unmistakable sense of natural closeness about the scene, and anyone would have said that they were plotting together.

As I quietly stepped away from the porch, I could hear my taxi carefully making its way through the darkness along the road leading to the house. Gatsby was still waiting in the driveway, exactly where I had left him.

"Is everything quiet up there?" he asked anxiously.

"Yes, everything is quiet." I paused. "You should come home and get some sleep."

He shook his head.

"I want to wait here until Daisy goes to bed. Good night, old sport."

He slipped his hands into his coat pockets and turned back with intense focus to his careful examination of the house, as if my being there somehow damaged the sacred nature of his watch. So I walked away and left him standing there in the moonlight— keeping guard over nothing.

Part 8

I couldn't sleep all night; a foghorn was moaning constantly on the Sound, and I lay restlessly, feeling half-sick as I drifted between bizarre reality and wild, terrifying dreams. Near dawn I heard a taxi driving up Gatsby's driveway, and right away I leaped out of bed and started getting dressed—I felt I had something important to tell him, something I needed to warn him about, and waiting until morning would be too late.

Crossing his lawn, I noticed that his front door remained open and he was slumped against a table in the hallway, weighed down by either despair or exhaustion.

"Nothing happened," he said weakly. "I waited, and around four o'clock she appeared at the window and stood there for a moment before turning off the light."

His house had never felt so massive to me as it did that evening when we searched through the vast rooms looking for cigarettes. We pulled back curtains that hung like enormous tents, and ran our hands along endless stretches of dark walls searching for light switches—at one point I stumbled with a kind of crash onto the keys of a spectral piano. There was a mysterious layer of dust covering everything, and the rooms smelled stale, as if they hadn't been opened to fresh air in many days. I discovered the cigar box on an unknown table, containing two old, dried-out cigarettes. Opening the French doors of the living room, we sat there smoking while looking out into the night.

"You should leave," I said. "They'll almost certainly track down your car."

"Go away now, old sport?"

"Go to Atlantic City for a week, or up to Montreal."

He refused to even think about it. There was no way he could leave Daisy until he found out what her plans were. He was holding onto one final thread of hope, and I couldn't bring myself to tear it away from him.

That night, he shared with me the unusual story of his youth with Dan Cody—he told me because "Jay Gatsby" had shattered like glass against Tom's cruel hatred, and the lengthy secret spectacle had come to an end. I believe he would have admitted to anything at that point, holding nothing back, but what he really wanted to discuss was Daisy.

She was the first "nice" girl he had ever encountered. Through various undisclosed roles, he had met such people before, but there had always been invisible barriers between them. He found her thrillingly attractive. He visited her home, initially with other officers from Camp Taylor, later by himself. It astonished him— he had never stepped foot in such a magnificent house before. But what filled it with an atmosphere of breathless intensity was that Daisy lived there—it was as ordinary to her as his tent at the camp was to him. There was a rich mystery surrounding it, a suggestion of bedrooms upstairs more lovely and refreshing than other bedrooms, of cheerful and glowing activities happening throughout its hallways, and of love affairs that were not stale and already stored away in lavender but vibrant and alive and fragrant with this year's gleaming automobiles and of parties whose flowers had barely begun to fade. It thrilled him as well that many men had previously loved Daisy—it enhanced her worth in his view. He sensed their presence throughout the house, filling the atmosphere with the shadows and remnants of emotions still pulsing with life.

But he understood that his presence in Daisy's house was purely due to an enormous stroke of luck. No matter how magnificent his destiny as Jay Gatsby might become, right now he was simply a broke young man with no history, and at any instant the protective disguise of his military uniform could fall away from him. Therefore, he seized every opportunity available to him. He grabbed whatever he could obtain, hungrily and without moral restraint—ultimately he claimed Daisy on a quiet October evening, claimed her precisely because he had no legitimate authority to even touch her hand.

He might have looked down on himself, since he had definitely brought her into his life through deception. I don't mean he had relied on his imaginary wealth, but he had purposely made Daisy feel safe and secure; he allowed her to think he came from the same social class as she did—that he could completely provide for and protect her. In reality, he lacked these resources—he didn't have a stable family supporting him, and he could be sent anywhere across the globe at any moment by an indifferent government.

But he didn't hate himself, and things didn't unfold the way he had pictured them. He had likely planned to take whatever he could get and leave—but now he discovered that he had bound himself to pursuing a holy grail. He understood that Daisy was remarkable, but he hadn't grasped just how remarkable a "proper" girl could turn out to be. She disappeared into her wealthy home, into her wealthy, abundant life, leaving Gatsby with nothing. He felt wedded to her, that was everything.

When they met again two days later, Gatsby was the one who seemed out of breath, the one who had somehow been let down. Her porch glowed with the expensive elegance of starlight; the wicker settee creaked stylishly as she turned to face him and he kissed her intriguing and beautiful lips. She had come down with a cold, which made her voice deeper and more enchanting than before, and Gatsby felt overwhelmed by the youth and mystery that money traps and protects, by the crispness of countless outfits, and by Daisy herself, shining like silver, secure and dignified above the desperate struggles of those without means.

"I can't tell you how shocked I was to discover that I loved her, old sport. I actually hoped for a time that she would break up with me, but she didn't, because she was in love with me as well. She believed I was knowledgeable because I understood different things than she did... Well, there I was, completely off track from my goals, falling deeper in love every moment, and suddenly I didn't care anymore. What was the point of accomplishing great things if I could have more fun telling her about what I planned to do?"

On the last afternoon before he left for overseas, he held Daisy in his arms for a long, quiet time. It was a chilly autumn day, with a fire burning in the room and her cheeks glowing pink. Every so often she shifted position and he adjusted his arm slightly, and at one point he kissed her dark, gleaming hair. The afternoon had brought them peace for a while, as if giving them a precious memory to carry through the long separation that tomorrow would bring. During their month together as lovers, they had never felt closer to each other, nor shared a deeper connection, than when she silently pressed her lips against his coat's shoulder or when he gently touched her fingertips, as softly as if she were sleeping.

He performed exceptionally well during the war. He held the rank of captain before being deployed to the front lines, and after the battles in the Argonne, he earned his promotion to major and was given command of the divisional machine guns. When the armistice was signed, he desperately tried to return home, but some confusion or miscommunication resulted in him being sent to Oxford instead. He was anxious at this point—Daisy's letters carried a tone of frantic desperation. She couldn't understand why he wasn't able to come back. She felt the weight of external pressures bearing down on her, and she longed to see him, to have him close by, and to gain the comfort that she was making the right choices.

Daisy was young, and her artificial world was filled with the scent of orchids and pleasant, cheerful snobbery, along with orchestras that set the rhythm of the year, capturing the sadness and suggestiveness of life in new melodies. Throughout the night, saxophones cried out the hopeless commentary of the "Beale Street Blues" while a hundred pairs of golden and silver slippers shuffled across the gleaming dust. During the grey tea hour, there were always rooms that pulsed continuously with this low, sweet fever, while fresh faces drifted here and there like rose petals carried by the melancholy horns around the dance floor.

Through this shadowy world, Daisy started moving again with the changing season; all at once she was back to juggling six appointments a day with six different men, and falling asleep at sunrise with the beads and delicate fabric of her evening gown twisted among wilting orchids scattered on the floor next to her bed. And constantly, something deep inside her was demanding a choice. She needed her life to take shape right now, this very moment—and the choice had to come from some powerful force—whether love, money, or undeniable practicality—that was within her reach.

That force materialized in the middle of spring when Tom Buchanan arrived on the scene. His presence carried a reassuring weight, both physically and socially, and Daisy found herself drawn to it. There was undoubtedly some internal conflict followed by a sense of resolution. The letter found its way to Gatsby while he remained at Oxford.

It was dawn now on Long Island and we went about opening the rest of the windows downstairs, filling the house with light that shifted from grey to gold. The shadow of a tree fell suddenly across the dew and ghostly birds began to sing among the blue leaves. There was a slow, pleasant movement in the air, barely a breeze, promising a cool, lovely day.

"I don't think she ever loved him." Gatsby turned away from the window and looked at me with a challenging expression. "You have to remember, old sport, she was extremely upset this afternoon. He said those things to her in a way that scared her—making it seem like I was nothing more than a common con artist. Because of that, she barely knew what she was saying."

He sat down with a heavy heart.

"Of course she might have loved him just for a minute, when they were first married—and loved me more even then, do you see?"

Suddenly he made a strange comment.

"In any case," he said, "it was just personal."

What could you make of that, other than to suspect there was some intensity in how he understood the situation that couldn't be quantified?

He returned from France while Tom and Daisy were still away on their honeymoon, and used the last of his military wages to make a heartbreaking yet compelling trip to Louisville. He spent a week there, wandering the same streets where their footsteps had echoed together during those November nights and returning to the secluded spots where they had driven in her white automobile. Just as Daisy's home had always appeared more enchanting and cheerful to him than any other residence, his perception of the entire city, even with her absence, remained filled with a sorrowful beauty.

He left with the feeling that if he had looked more thoroughly, he might have discovered her—that he was abandoning her. The day coach—he had no money left now—was sweltering. He walked out to the open platform and settled into a folding chair, watching the station glide past and the rear sides of unknown buildings drift by. Then they moved into the spring countryside, where a yellow streetcar raced alongside them briefly, carrying passengers who might have once glimpsed the ethereal beauty of her face on some ordinary street.

The track curved and now it was moving away from the sun, which, as it dropped lower, appeared to spread itself like a blessing over the disappearing city where she had lived and breathed. He reached out his hand frantically as if to catch just a breath of air, to preserve a piece of the place that she had made beautiful for him. But everything was passing by too quickly now for his clouded vision and he realized that he had lost that part of it, the most vibrant and precious, forever.

It was nine o'clock when we finished breakfast and stepped out onto the porch. The night had brought a dramatic change in the weather, and there was an autumn feeling in the air. The gardener, the last remaining member of Gatsby's former staff, approached the bottom of the steps.

"I'm going to drain the pool today, Mr. Gatsby. The leaves will start falling soon, and then we always have problems with the pipes."

"Don't do it today," Gatsby replied. He turned to me with an apologetic look. "You know, old sport, I haven't used that pool once all summer."

I glanced at my watch and got to my feet.

"Twelve minutes to my train."

I didn't want to go to the city. I wasn't capable of doing any decent work, but there was more to it than that—I didn't want to leave Gatsby behind. I missed that train, and then missed another one, before I could finally bring myself to leave.

"I'll call you," I said finally.

"Do, old sport."

"I'll call you around noon."

We walked slowly down the steps.

"I suppose Daisy will call too." He looked at me anxiously, as if he hoped I would corroborate this.

"I suppose so."

"Well, goodbye."

We shook hands and I began to leave. Right before I got to the hedge I remembered something and turned around.

"They're a rotten crowd," I shouted across the lawn. "You're worth the whole damn bunch put together."

I've always been happy I said that. It was the only kind thing I ever said to him, since I disapproved of everything about him from start to finish. At first he gave a courteous nod, then his face lit up with that brilliant and knowing smile, as though we had been secretly sharing that understanding all along. His beautiful pink wreck of a suit created a vivid splash of color against the white steps, and I remembered the evening when I first arrived at his family estate three months earlier. The lawn and driveway had been packed with the faces of people who suspected his dishonesty—and there he had stood on those very steps, hiding his pure dream, as he waved farewell to them.

I expressed my gratitude for his generous hospitality. We constantly found ourselves thanking him for this kindness—myself and the rest of the group.

"Goodbye," I called out. "I really enjoyed breakfast, Gatsby."

———————

Up in the city, I spent some time trying to record stock quotes for an endless number of shares, then I dozed off in my swivel chair. Shortly before noon, the telephone woke me up, and I jerked awake with perspiration forming on my forehead. It was Jordan Baker calling; she frequently phoned me around this time because her unpredictable schedule of moving between hotels, clubs, and private homes made her difficult to reach any other way. Typically her voice sounded fresh and cool over the phone line, like a piece of turf from a lush golf course had floated through the office window, but this morning her voice sounded rough and parched.

"I've left Daisy's house," she said. "I'm at Hempstead, and I'm going down to Southampton this afternoon."

Leaving Daisy's house was probably the tactful thing to do, but doing so irritated me, and what she said next made me tense up completely.

"You weren't so nice to me last night."

"How could it have mattered then?"

Silence for a moment. Then:

"However—I want to see you."

"I want to see you, too."

"What if I skip Southampton and come into the city this afternoon instead?"

"No—I don't think this afternoon."

"Very well."

"I can't do it this afternoon. There are various—"

We chatted like that for some time, and then suddenly we stopped talking altogether. I'm not sure which one of us ended the call with that harsh click, but I know it didn't matter to me. I wouldn't have been able to have a conversation with her face-to-face that day, even if it meant never speaking to her again for the rest of my life.

I called Gatsby's house a few minutes later, but the phone line was busy. I tried four times; finally a frustrated operator told me the line was being kept open for a long-distance call from Detroit. I pulled out my train schedule and drew a small circle around the three-fifty departure. Then I leaned back in my chair and tried to think. It was exactly noon.

When I rode past the ash-heaps on the train that morning, I had deliberately moved to the opposite side of the car. I figured there would be a crowd of curious onlookers gathered there all day, with young boys hunting for dark stains in the dirt, and some talkative man repeating the story over and over until it gradually became less real even to him and he could no longer bring himself to tell it, and Myrtle Wilson's tragic end would be forgotten. Now I want to step back a bit and describe what took place at the garage after we departed there the previous night.

They struggled to find the sister, Catherine. She must have abandoned her usual rule against drinking that evening, because when she showed up she was dazed from alcohol and couldn't grasp that the ambulance had already departed for Flushing. Once they managed to make her understand this, she collapsed immediately, as though this detail was the unbearable aspect of the whole situation. Someone, whether out of kindness or curiosity, helped her into his car and followed behind her sister's body.

Until well past midnight, a shifting crowd gathered outside the garage entrance, while George Wilson sat inside, rocking back and forth on the couch. The office door remained open for some time, and every person who entered the garage couldn't help but look through it. Eventually someone remarked that it wasn't right, and shut the door. Michaelis stayed with Wilson along with several other men; initially there were four or five, then the number dropped to two or three. Later on, Michaelis had to ask the final stranger to remain for another fifteen minutes while he returned to his own place to brew some coffee. Following that, he remained alone with Wilson until daybreak.

Around three o'clock, Wilson's rambling speech shifted—he became calmer and started discussing the yellow car. He declared that he knew how to discover who owned the yellow car, and then he suddenly revealed that a few months earlier his wife had returned from the city with a bruised face and swollen nose.

But when he heard himself say this, he winced and started crying "Oh, my God!" again in his anguished voice. Michaelis made an awkward attempt to distract him.

"How long have you been married, George? Come on, try to sit still for a minute and answer my question. How long have you been married?"

"Twelve years."

"Have you ever had any children? Come on, George, sit still— I asked you a question. Did you ever have any children?"

The hard brown beetles continued banging against the dim light, and every time Michaelis heard a car racing down the road outside, it reminded him of the car that had failed to stop just a few hours earlier. He avoided going into the garage because the workbench bore stains from where the body had lain, so he paced restlessly around the office—he had memorized every item in it by dawn—and occasionally sat down next to Wilson, attempting to keep him calm.

"Do you have a church you attend sometimes, George? Even if you haven't been there in a while? Maybe I could contact the church and ask a priest to come visit so he could speak with you, you know?"

"Don't belong to any."

"You should have a church, George, for moments like this. You must have attended church at some point. Weren't you married in a church? Listen, George, listen to what I'm saying. Weren't you married in a church?"

"That was a long time ago."

The effort of responding disrupted the steady rhythm of his rocking motion—for a moment he fell silent. Then the same expression returned to his weary eyes, one that seemed caught between partial understanding and complete confusion.

"Look in the drawer over there," he said, pointing at the desk.

"Which drawer?"

"That drawer—that one."

Michaelis pulled open the drawer closest to him. Inside, there was nothing except a small, costly dog leash crafted from leather and woven silver. It looked brand new.

"This?" he asked, holding it up.

Wilson stared and nodded.

"I discovered it yesterday afternoon. She attempted to explain it to me, but I could tell something was strange about it."

"You mean your wife bought it?"

"She had it wrapped in tissue paper on her dresser."

Michaelis found nothing strange about it and offered Wilson twelve different explanations for why his wife might have purchased the dog leash. However, Wilson had likely heard some of these very same justifications before from Myrtle, because he started whispering "Oh, my God!" once more—his consoler abandoned several explanations unfinished.

"Then he killed her," Wilson said. His mouth suddenly fell open.

"Who did?"

"I have a way of finding out."

"You're being morbid, George," his friend said. "This whole situation has been stressful for you, and you don't realize what you're saying. You should try to sit quietly until morning."

"He murdered her."

"It was an accident, George."

Wilson shook his head. His eyes grew narrow and his mouth widened just a bit with the hint of a condescending "Hm!"

"I know," he said with certainty. "I'm one of those trusting guys and I don't think badly of anyone, but when I figure something out, I really know it. It was the man in that car. She ran out to talk to him and he wouldn't stop."

Michaelis had noticed this as well, but he hadn't thought there was anything particularly meaningful about it. He assumed that

Mrs. Wilson had been fleeing from her husband, rather than attempting to flag down a specific car.

"How could she have been like that?"

"She's a deep one," said Wilson, as if that answered the question. "Ah-h-h—"

He started rocking back and forth again, while Michaelis stood there twisting the leash in his hand.

"Maybe you have a friend I could call for you, George?"

This was a desperate hope—he felt almost certain that Wilson had no friend: there wasn't enough of him even for his wife. He felt somewhat relieved a little later when he observed a change in the room, a blue brightening near the window, and understood that dawn was approaching. Around five o'clock it was bright enough outside to turn off the light.

Wilson's vacant eyes gazed out toward the ash-heaps, where small gray clouds formed strange shapes and hurried back and forth in the gentle morning breeze.

"I talked to her," he mumbled after a lengthy pause. "I told her she could deceive me, but she couldn't deceive God. I brought her over to the window"—struggling, he stood up and made his way to the back window, pressing his face against the glass—"and I said 'God sees what you've been up to, everything you've been doing. You might be able to trick me, but you can't trick God!'"

Standing behind him, Michaelis was shocked to see that he was staring at the eyes of Doctor T. J. Eckleburg, which had just appeared, pale and massive, from the fading night.

"God sees everything," Wilson said again.

"That's just an advertisement," Michaelis told him with certainty. Something compelled him to turn away from the window and glance back into the room. Wilson, however, remained standing there for quite some time, his face pressed close to the glass, nodding as he stared out into the fading evening light.

By six o'clock, Michaelis was exhausted and relieved to hear a car pull up outside. One of the men who had kept watch the night before had returned as promised, so Michaelis prepared breakfast for three people, which he and the other man shared. Wilson had grown quieter by then, and Michaelis left for home to get some sleep; when he woke up four hours later and rushed back to the garage, Wilson had disappeared.

His movements—he walked everywhere—were later tracked to Port Roosevelt and then to Gad's Hill, where he purchased a sandwich he never ate and a cup of coffee. He must have been exhausted and moving at a slow pace, since he didn't arrive at Gad's Hill until noon. Up to this point, accounting for his whereabouts wasn't difficult—there were boys who had witnessed a man "behaving kind of strangely," and drivers whom he stared at peculiarly from the roadside. Then for three hours he vanished completely. The police, based on what he told Michaelis about having "a way of finding out," assumed he spent those hours going from one garage to another in the area, asking about a yellow car. However, no garage owner who might have encountered him ever stepped forward, and perhaps he had a simpler, more reliable method of discovering what he needed to know. By two-thirty he was in West Egg, where he asked someone for directions to Gatsby's house. So by that point he knew Gatsby's name.

At two o'clock, Gatsby changed into his swimming attire and told the butler that if anyone called, he should be notified at the pool. He went to the garage to get an air mattress that had entertained his guests throughout the summer, and his driver assisted him in inflating it. He then ordered that the convertible should not be driven under any conditions—which was odd, since the front right fender required fixing.

156

Gatsby lifted the mattress onto his shoulder and headed toward the pool. He paused once to adjust his grip slightly, and the chauffeur offered to help him, but he declined with a shake of his head and soon vanished among the trees that were turning yellow.

No telephone message arrived, but the butler stayed awake and waited for it until four o'clock—until long after there was no one left to deliver it to if it had come. I believe that Gatsby himself didn't think it would come, and maybe he didn't care anymore. If that was the case, he must have felt that he had lost the old comfortable world, paying a steep price for living too long with a single dream. He must have gazed up at a strange sky through terrifying leaves and trembled as he discovered what a hideous thing a rose is and how harsh the sunlight was on the barely formed grass. A new world, physical without being genuine, where unfortunate spirits, breathing dreams like air, wandered randomly about... like that gray, surreal figure moving toward him through the shapeless trees.

The driver—he was one of Wolfshiem's associates—heard the gunshots—later he could only say that he hadn't thought much about them. I drove straight from the station to Gatsby's house and my hurried, worried rush up the front steps was the first thing that made anyone realize something was wrong. But I'm certain they knew then. With barely a word spoken, the four of us—the driver, butler, gardener, and I—rushed down to the pool.

There was a subtle, almost invisible movement in the water as the fresh current from one side pushed its way toward the drain on the opposite end. With tiny ripples that barely resembled waves, the weighted mattress drifted unevenly across the pool. A gentle breeze that barely wrinkled the surface was sufficient to alter its random path with its unintended cargo. The contact with a group of leaves turned it slowly, drawing, like the arm of a compass, a narrow red circle in the water.

157

It was after we began walking with Gatsby toward the house that the gardener discovered Wilson's body lying some distance away in the grass, and the tragedy was complete.

Part 9

After two years, I can only recall the remainder of that day, along with that night and the following day, as a relentless parade of police officers, photographers, and reporters streaming in and out through Gatsby's front entrance. A rope had been strung across the main gate with a policeman stationed there to keep away the curious onlookers, but small boys quickly figured out they could slip through my yard, and there were always several of them gathered around the pool with their mouths hanging open. Someone speaking with confident authority, possibly a detective, used the word "madman" while examining Wilson's body that afternoon, and the casual certainty in his tone established the narrative for the newspaper stories that appeared the next morning.

Most of those reports were a complete nightmare—bizarre, detailed, sensational, and completely false. When Michaelis testified at the inquest and revealed Wilson's suspicions about his wife, I expected the entire story would soon be turned into scandalous gossip—but Catherine, who could have said anything, remained completely silent. She displayed remarkable strength of character too—stared at the coroner with resolute eyes beneath that reshaped eyebrow of hers, and testified under oath that her sister had never met Gatsby, that her sister was perfectly content with her husband, that her sister hadn't been involved in any wrongdoing whatsoever. She managed to convince herself of this, and wept into her handkerchief, as though the mere suggestion was unbearable. So Wilson was simply labeled a man "driven mad by grief" so that the case could stay as straightforward as possible. And that's where it remained.

But all of this seemed distant and unimportant. I found myself standing with Gatsby, completely alone. From the moment I called

West Egg village to report the tragedy, everyone directed their questions and assumptions about him to me. Initially, I felt surprised and bewildered; then, as he lay motionless in his house, unable to move, breathe, or speak, hour after hour, I gradually realized that I had become responsible for him, simply because no one else cared—cared, that is, with the kind of deep personal concern that everyone deserves to have someone show them when their life comes to an end.

I phoned Daisy thirty minutes after we discovered him, calling her automatically and without any doubt. However, she and Tom had left earlier that afternoon, taking their luggage with them.

"Didn't leave an address?"

"No."

"Did they say when they'd be back?"

"No."

"Do you have any idea where they might be? How I could get in touch with them?"

"I don't know. Can't say."

I wanted to find someone for him. I wanted to go into the room where he was lying and comfort him: "I'll find someone for you, Gatsby. Don't worry. Just trust me and I'll find someone for you—"

Meyer Wolfshiem's name wasn't listed in the phone book. The butler provided me with his office address on Broadway, so I contacted Information for the number, but by the time I received it, it was well past five o'clock, and nobody picked up the phone.

"Will you ring again?"

"I've rung three times."

"It's very important."

"Sorry. I'm afraid no one's there."

I returned to the drawing room and for a moment thought these were random visitors—all these official people who had suddenly crowded into the space. But even though they pulled back the sheet and stared at Gatsby with horrified expressions, his objection kept echoing in my mind:

"Listen, my friend, you need to find someone to help me. You have to make a real effort. I can't handle this by myself."

Someone began asking me questions, but I pulled away and hurried upstairs to quickly search through the unlocked sections of his desk—he had never clearly told me that his parents were dead. However, there was nothing there—only the photograph of Dan Cody, a reminder of past violence, looking down from the wall.

The next morning I sent the butler to New York carrying a letter for Wolfshiem that requested information and pressed him to take the next train out. The request felt unnecessary as I wrote it. I felt certain he would come immediately upon seeing the newspapers, just as I felt certain a telegram from Daisy would arrive before noon—but no telegram came, nor did Mr. Wolfshiem; nobody came except additional police officers, photographers, and reporters. When the butler returned with Wolfshiem's response, I began to feel defiant, sensing a contemptuous bond between Gatsby and myself against all of them.

Dear Mr. Carraway.

This has been one of the most devastating shocks of my life and I can barely believe that any of it is real. Such an insane act as that man committed should give us all pause for thought.

I cannot come down right now because I am caught up in some very important business and cannot afford to get involved in this situation at the moment.

If there is anything I can do later on, please let me know in a letter through Edgar. I hardly know what to think when I hear about something like this and feel completely overwhelmed and defeated.

Yours truly
Meyer Wolfshiem

and then hurried additions written below:

Let me know about the funeral and other arrangements since I don't know his family at all.

When the phone rang that afternoon and Long Distance announced that Chicago was calling, I assumed it would finally be Daisy. However, when the connection went through, I heard a man's voice that sounded very thin and distant.

"This is Slagle speaking…"

"Yes?" The name was unfamiliar.

"What a terrible situation, isn't it? Did you get my telegram?"

"There haven't been any wires."

"Young Parke's in trouble," he said quickly. "They arrested him when he passed the bonds across the counter. They received a notice from New York with the serial numbers just five minutes earlier. What do you make of that? You can never predict what will happen in these small towns—"

"Hello!" I interrupted, out of breath. "Listen—this isn't Mr. Gatsby. Mr. Gatsby's dead."

There was a long silence on the other end of the line, followed by an exclamation… then a quick squawk as the connection was broken.

———————————

I believe it was on the third day when a telegram signed by Henry C. Gatz arrived from a town in Minnesota. The message simply stated that the sender was departing immediately and requested that the funeral be postponed until his arrival.

It was Gatsby's father, a serious elderly man who appeared utterly lost and confused, wrapped in a long, inexpensive overcoat despite the warm September weather. Tears streamed down his face constantly from his overwhelming emotions, and when I relieved him of his bag and umbrella, he started tugging relentlessly at his thin gray beard, making it challenging for me to help him remove his coat. He seemed ready to collapse at any moment, so I guided him to the music room and had him sit down while I arranged for some food to be brought. However, he refused to eat, and the glass of milk slipped from his shaking hands and spilled.

"I saw it in the Chicago newspaper," he said. "It was all in the Chicago newspaper. I started right away."

"I didn't know how to reach you."

His eyes, unable to see anything, moved restlessly around the room.

"It was a madman," he said. "He must have been mad."

"Would you like some coffee?" I asked him.

"I don't want anything. I'm all right now, Mr.—"

"Carraway."

"Well, I'm all right now. Where have they got Jimmy?"

I brought him into the living room where his son was lying and left him there. A few young boys had gathered on the front steps and were peering into the hallway; when I informed them who had come, they departed with reluctance.

After a short time, Mr. Gatz opened the door and stepped out, his mouth hanging open, his face slightly red, his eyes shedding scattered and irregular tears. He had reached an age where death no longer carried the shock of something horrifying and unexpected, and when he looked around for the first time and noticed the impressive height and magnificence of the entrance hall and the grand rooms that extended from it into additional rooms, his sorrow started to blend with amazed pride. I guided him to a bedroom on the upper floor; while he removed his coat and vest, I explained to him that all the preparations had been postponed until his arrival.

"I didn't know what you'd want, Mr. Gatsby—"

"Gatz is my name."

"—Mr. Gatz. I thought you might want to take the body West."

He shook his head.

"Jimmy always preferred it back East. He worked his way up to his position in the East. Were you a friend of my boy's, Mr.—?"

"We were close friends."

"He had a bright future ahead of him, you know. He was just a young man, but he possessed tremendous intelligence."

He touched his head in an impressive manner, and I nodded.

"If he had lived, he would have been a great man. A man like James J. Hill. He would have helped build up the country."

"That's true," I said, feeling uncomfortable.

He struggled with the embroidered bedspread, attempting to pull it off the bed, then lay down rigidly and fell asleep immediately.

That night someone who was clearly scared called, and insisted on knowing who I was before they would tell me their name.

"This is Mr. Carraway," I said.

"Oh!" He sounded relieved. "This is Klipspringer."

I felt relieved as well, since this appeared to guarantee another friend would be present at Gatsby's burial. I didn't want the news to appear in the newspapers and attract curious onlookers, so I had been personally contacting several people. They proved difficult to locate.

"The funeral is tomorrow," I said. "Three o'clock, here at the house. I wish you would tell anyone who might be interested."

"Oh, I will," he said quickly. "Of course I probably won't see anyone, but if I do."

His tone made me suspicious.

"Of course you'll be there yourself."

"Well, I'll definitely give it a shot. What I'm calling about is—"

"Hold on," I interrupted. "What about saying you'll come?"

"Well, the truth is—the reality of the situation is that I'm staying with some people here in Greenwich, and they're expecting me to be with them tomorrow. Actually, there's some kind of picnic or gathering planned. Of course I'll do everything I can to get away."

I let out an uncontrolled "Huh!" and he must have heard me, because he continued nervously:

"I'm calling about a pair of shoes I left at your place. I was wondering if it would be too much trouble to have your butler send them to me. They're tennis shoes, and I really need them. You can send them to me care of B. F.—"

I didn't catch the rest of the name because I hung up the phone.

After that, I felt ashamed for Gatsby—one man I called on the phone suggested that he had gotten what was coming to him. But that was my mistake, since he was one of those people who used to mock Gatsby most harshly while drinking Gatsby's alcohol, and I should have known better than to contact him.

On the morning of the funeral, I traveled up to New York to meet with Meyer Wolfshiem; I couldn't find any other way to get in touch with him. Following the elevator operator's directions, I pushed open a door marked "The Swastika Holding Company," and initially it appeared no one was there. After I called out "hello" multiple times without response, I heard an argument erupt from behind a divider, and soon a beautiful Jewish woman emerged from an inner doorway and examined me with dark, unfriendly eyes.

"Nobody's in," she said. "Mr. Wolfshiem's gone to Chicago."

The first part of this was clearly false, since someone had started whistling "The Rosary" off-key from inside.

"Please tell him that Mr. Carraway would like to see him."

"I can't get him back from Chicago, can I?"

At that moment, a voice that was unmistakably Wolfshiem's called out "Stella!" from the other side of the door.

"Write your name on the desk," she said quickly. "I'll give it to him when he returns."

"But I know he's there."

She moved closer to me and started running her hands up and down her hips in an indignant manner.

"You young men think you can just barge in here whenever you want," she scolded. "We're getting absolutely sick of it. When I tell you he's in Chicago, he's in Chicago."

I mentioned Gatsby.

"Oh!" She looked me over once more. "Would you just— What did you say your name was?"

She disappeared. Within moments, Meyer Wolfshiem appeared solemnly in the doorway, extending both hands toward me. He guided me into his office, commenting in a respectful tone that this was a difficult time for everyone, and he offered me a cigar.

"I remember when I first met him," he said. "He was a young major fresh out of the military, decorated with war medals. He was so broke that he had to keep wearing his uniform since he couldn't afford to buy civilian clothes. The first time I saw him was when he walked into Winebrenner's pool hall on Forty-third Street looking for work. He hadn't eaten anything for several days. 'Come on, let me buy you lunch,' I told him. He consumed more than four dollars' worth of food in thirty minutes."

"Did you help him get started in business?" I asked.

"Start him! I made him."

"Oh."

"I lifted him up from nothing, straight out of the gutter. I could tell immediately that he was a good-looking, well-mannered young man, and when he mentioned he had been to Oxford I knew he would be useful to me. I convinced him to join the

166

American Legion where he earned a respected position. Almost right away he handled some business for one of my clients up in Albany. We were as close as this in everything"—he raised two thick fingers—"always side by side."

I wondered if this partnership had been involved in the World Series scandal of 1919.

"Now he's dead," I said after a moment. "You were his closest friend, so I know you'll want to come to his funeral this afternoon."

"I'd like to come."

"Well, come then."

The hair in his nostrils trembled gently, and when he shook his head, his eyes welled up with tears.

"I can't do it—I can't get mixed up in it," he said.

"There's nothing to get mixed up in. It's all over now."

"When someone gets killed, I never want to get involved in any way. I stay out of it. When I was younger, things were different—if a friend of mine died, regardless of how it happened, I stayed with them until the end. You might think that sounds sentimental, but I'm serious—right to the very end."

I could see that for whatever reason, he had made up his mind not to come, so I got to my feet.

"Are you a college graduate?" he asked suddenly.

For a moment I thought he was going to suggest a "connection," but he only nodded and shook my hand.

"Let's learn to show our friendship for someone while they're still alive, not after they've died," he suggested. "After that, my own rule is to leave everything as it is."

When I left his office, the sky had grown dark and I returned to West Egg in a light rain. After I changed my clothes, I went next door and discovered Mr. Gatz pacing back and forth with excitement in the hallway. His pride in his son and his son's belongings kept growing stronger, and now he had something he wanted to show me.

"Jimmy sent me this picture." He pulled out his wallet with shaking fingers. "Take a look at this."

It was a photograph of the house, with cracked corners and smudged from being handled by countless people. He enthusiastically pointed out every detail to me. "Look there!" he said, then searched my face for signs of admiration. He had displayed it so frequently that I believe the photograph had become more real to him than the actual house itself.

"Jimmy sent it to me. I think it's a very pretty picture. It shows up well."

"Very well. Had you seen him lately?"

"He came out to see me two years ago and bought me the house I'm living in now. Of course we had broken up when he ran away from home, but I can see now there was a reason for it. He knew he had a bright future ahead of him. And ever since he became successful he has been very generous with me."

He appeared hesitant to put the picture away, holding it for another moment, lingering before my eyes. Then he put the wallet back and pulled a worn old copy of a book called Hopalong Cassidy from his pocket.

"Look, this is a book he owned when he was a child. It really shows you something."

He opened it to the back cover and turned it around so I could see. On the final flyleaf, the word "schedule" was printed along with the date September 12, 1906. Below that:

Rise from bed	6:00a.m.
Dumbell exercise and wall-scaling	6:15–6:30
Study electricity, etc.	7:15–8:15
Work	8:30–4:30p.m.
Baseball and sports	4:30–5:00
Practise elocution, poise and how to attain it	5:00–6:00
Study needed inventions	7:00–9:00

General Resolves

- No wasting time at Shafters or [a name, indecipherable]
- No more smoking or chewing.
- Bathe every other day
- Read one self-improvement book or magazine each week
- Save $5.00 $3.00 per week
- Be better to your parents

"I stumbled upon this book by chance," the elderly man said. "It just goes to show, doesn't it?"

"It just shows you."

"Jimmy was destined to succeed. He always had resolutions like this or similar ones. Do you see what he's written about bettering his mind? He was always passionate about that. He once told me I ate like a pig, and I beat him for saying it."

He didn't want to close the book, reading each item out loud and then looking at me with anticipation. I believe he was hoping I would write down the list for myself.

A little before three o'clock, the Lutheran minister arrived from Flushing, and I found myself automatically glancing out the windows, searching for other cars. Gatsby's father did the same thing. As time went by and the servants entered the room to stand waiting in the hallway, his eyes started blinking nervously, and he talked about the rain with worry and uncertainty in his voice. The minister checked his watch multiple times, so I pulled him aside and requested that he wait another half hour. However, it made no difference. No one showed up.

Around five o'clock, our small convoy of three vehicles arrived at the cemetery and came to a halt in the steady drizzle next to the entrance gate. Leading the way was a motor hearse, ominously black and glistening with rain, followed by Mr. Gatz, the minister, and myself in the limousine. Behind us, four or five servants and the West Egg postman rode in Gatsby's station wagon, all of them soaked through to the skin. As we began making our way through the cemetery gate, I heard the sound of another car pulling up, followed by the splash of footsteps hurrying across the waterlogged ground behind us. When I turned to look, I saw it was the man with the owl-like glasses—the same person I had discovered admiring Gatsby's book collection in the library that evening three months earlier.

I hadn't seen him since that time. I have no idea how he found out about the funeral, or what his name was. Rain streamed down his thick glasses, so he removed them and cleaned them off to get a better look at the protective canvas being pulled away from Gatsby's grave.

I attempted to focus my thoughts on Gatsby for a brief moment, but he had already drifted too far into the distance, and I could only recall, without any bitterness, that Daisy had failed to send even a message or a single flower. Faintly I heard someone whisper "Blessed are the dead that the rain falls on," and then the man with owl-like eyes responded "Amen to that," speaking with a courageous voice.

We hurried down through the rain to the cars, moving in a scattered group. Owl-eyes approached me at the gate and began to speak.

"I couldn't get to the house," he remarked.

"Nobody else could either."

"Keep going!" he said, startled. "Good God! Hundreds of people used to go there."

He removed his glasses and cleaned them once more, both the outer and inner surfaces of the lenses.

"The poor son-of-a-bitch," he said.

One of my clearest memories involves returning West from prep school and later from college during Christmas break. Those of us traveling beyond Chicago would meet at the old, dimly lit Union Station at six o'clock on a December evening, accompanied by a few Chicago friends who were already swept up in their own holiday celebrations, ready to say quick goodbyes. I recall the fur coats worn by girls coming back from Miss This-or-That's school and the chatter visible in frozen breath and hands waving above our heads as we spotted familiar faces, along with the exchange of invitations: "Are you going to the Ordways'? the Herseys'? the Schultzes'?" and the long green tickets gripped tightly in our gloved hands. Finally, there were the dark yellow cars of the Chicago, Milwaukee and St. Paul railroad that appeared as cheerful as Christmas itself on the tracks next to the gate.

When we departed into the winter night and the genuine snow, our own snow, started to extend alongside us and sparkle against the windows, and the faint lights of little Wisconsin stations passed by, a crisp wild invigoration suddenly filled the air. We breathed it in deeply as we made our way back from dinner through the chilly connecting passages, profoundly conscious of our connection with this land for one remarkable hour, before we dissolved seamlessly back into it once more.

That's my Middle West—not the wheat fields or the prairies or the forgotten Swedish towns, but the exciting homecoming trains of my youth, and the streetlights and sleigh bells in the cold darkness and the silhouettes of holly wreaths cast by illuminated windows onto the snow. I belong to that world, somewhat serious from experiencing those long winters, somewhat self-satisfied from being raised in the Carraway house in a city where homes are still known for decades by their family's name. I understand now that this has been a story of the West, after all—Tom and Gatsby, Daisy and Jordan and I, were all Westerners, and perhaps we shared some common shortcoming that made us quietly unsuited to Eastern life.

Even when the East thrilled me most, even when I was most acutely conscious of how much better it was than the bored, sprawling, bloated cities beyond the Ohio, with their endless interrogations that only spared children and the elderly—even then it always had a twisted quality for me. West Egg, in particular, still appears in my most surreal dreams. I picture it as a nighttime scene painted by El Greco: a hundred houses, both ordinary and bizarre at the same time, hunched beneath a dark, looming sky and a dull moon. In the front, four serious men wearing formal suits walk along the sidewalk carrying a stretcher that holds a drunk woman dressed in a white evening gown. Her hand, hanging over the edge, glitters coldly with jewelry. The men solemnly turn into a house—the wrong house. But nobody knows the woman's name, and nobody cares.

After Gatsby died, the East became haunted for me in that same way, twisted beyond what my eyes could fix or make right. So when the blue smoke from dry, crumbling leaves filled the air and the wind made the damp laundry rigid on the clothesline, I decided to return home.

There was one thing I needed to do before leaving, something awkward and unpleasant that probably should have been left alone. But I wanted to set things straight and not simply rely on that accommodating and indifferent ocean to wash away my mess. I met with Jordan Baker and we discussed what had occurred between us, and what had taken place in my life since then, while she remained completely motionless, listening, in a large chair.

She was dressed for golf, and I remember thinking she looked like a perfect picture, her chin lifted with a touch of confidence, her hair the color of an autumn leaf, her face the same brown shade as the fingerless glove resting on her knee. When I finished speaking, she told me matter-of-factly that she was engaged to another man. I had my doubts about that, even though there were several men she could have married with just a nod, but I acted surprised. For a brief moment I wondered if I was making a mistake, then I quickly thought everything through again and stood up to say goodbye.

"But you still dumped me," Jordan said out of nowhere. "You broke up with me over the phone. I don't care about you anymore, but that was something I'd never experienced before, and it left me feeling off-balance for a while."

We shook hands.

"Oh, and do you remember," she added, "a conversation we had once about driving a car?"

"Why—not exactly."

"You said a bad driver was only safe until she met another bad driver? Well, I met another bad driver, didn't I? I mean it was careless of me to make such a wrong guess. I thought you were rather an honest, straightforward person. I thought it was your secret pride."

"I'm thirty," I said. "I'm five years too old to lie to myself and call it honor."

She didn't respond. Furious, partly infatuated with her, and deeply regretful, I turned away.

One afternoon late in October, I spotted Tom Buchanan. He was striding ahead of me down Fifth Avenue with his characteristic alert, aggressive manner, his hands positioned slightly away from his body as though ready to ward off any obstruction, his head turning quickly from side to side, following the movement of his restless eyes. Just as I reduced my pace to prevent catching up with him, he came to a halt and started staring intently into the display windows of a jewelry store. All at once he noticed me and approached, extending his hand toward me.

"What's wrong, Nick? Do you have a problem shaking hands with me?"

"Yes. You know what I think of you."

"You're crazy, Nick," he said quickly. "Completely insane. I have no idea what's wrong with you."

"Tom," I asked, "what did you say to Wilson that afternoon?"

He looked at me in complete silence, and I realized I had correctly figured out what happened during those unaccounted hours. I began to walk away, but he moved forward and seized my arm.

"I told him the truth," he said. "He showed up at the door while we were preparing to leave, and when I sent word down that we weren't home, he tried to push his way up the stairs. He was insane enough to murder me if I hadn't revealed who owned the car. His hand stayed on a gun in his pocket the entire time he was in the house—" He stopped speaking with defiance. "So what if I told him? That guy deserved what he got. He fooled you just like he fooled Daisy, but he was a ruthless man. He struck Myrtle with his car like you'd hit a dog and didn't even bother to stop."

There was nothing I could say, except for the one unspeakable truth that it wasn't accurate.

"And if you think I didn't experience my fair share of pain— look, when I went to give up that apartment and saw that damned box of dog biscuits sitting there on the sideboard, I sat down and cried like a child. My God, it was terrible—"

I couldn't forgive him or find any affection for him, but I understood that in his mind, everything he had done was completely justified. The whole situation was reckless and chaotic. Tom and Daisy were thoughtless individuals—they destroyed things and people's lives, then withdrew into their wealth or their enormous indifference, or whatever force held their relationship together, leaving others to deal with the wreckage they had created...

I shook hands with him; it seemed foolish not to, since I suddenly felt as though I were speaking with a child. Then he walked into the jewelry store to purchase a pearl necklace—or maybe just a pair of cufflinks—freed from my small-town prudishness forever.

Gatsby's house remained vacant when I departed—the grass on his lawn had grown just as tall as mine. One of the local taxi drivers never passed the entrance gate with a passenger without pausing for a moment to point toward the property; maybe he was the one who had driven Daisy and Gatsby to East Egg on the night of the crash, and maybe he had created his own version of what happened. I had no desire to listen to his account and I stayed away from him whenever I stepped off the train.

I spent my Saturday nights in New York because those brilliant, sparkling parties of his remained so vivid in my memory that I could still hear the music and laughter, soft and continuous, drifting from his garden, along with the sound of cars moving up and down his driveway. One evening I actually heard a real car there and watched its headlights come to a stop at his front entrance. However, I chose not to look into it. It was probably some last guest who had been traveling in distant places and had no idea that the party had ended.

On the final night, with my suitcase packed and my car sold to the local grocer, I walked over to take one last look at that enormous, chaotic disaster of a house. On the white front steps, someone had scratched a vulgar word with a piece of brick, and it showed up starkly in the moonlight, so I rubbed it out by scraping my shoe roughly across the stone. Afterward, I made my way down to the beach and stretched out on the sand.

Most of the large waterfront resorts had shut down for the season, and barely any lights remained visible except for the dim, shifting glow from a ferry making its way across the Sound. As the moon climbed higher in the sky, the unnecessary houses seemed to fade from view until I slowly realized I was looking at the ancient island that had once bloomed before the eyes of Dutch sailors—a vibrant, green promise of the new world. The vanished trees that had once stood here, the same trees that had been cleared to make room for Gatsby's mansion, had once whispered seductively about the final and most magnificent of all human aspirations; for one brief, magical moment, humanity must have caught its breath while standing before this continent, drawn into a kind of beautiful reflection that they couldn't fully grasp or even wanted, coming face to face for the final time in human history with something that matched their infinite capacity for amazement.

As I sat there contemplating the ancient, mysterious world, I reflected on Gatsby's amazement when he first spotted the green light at the end of Daisy's pier. He had traveled such a great distance to reach this blue lawn, and his dream must have appeared so near that he could barely miss catching it. He was unaware that it had already passed him by, somewhere back in that enormous darkness beyond the city, where the shadowy fields of the republic stretched endlessly beneath the night sky.

Gatsby had faith in the green light, the ecstatic future that retreats from us year after year. It escaped our grasp back then, but that doesn't matter—tomorrow we'll run with greater speed, extend our arms even farther… And on one beautiful morning—

So we keep pushing forward, like boats fighting against the current, constantly pulled back into what came before.

THE END

Thank You For Reading

You've Just Read a Piece of the Greatest Library Ever Rebuilt

Thank you for reading.

This book is one of thousands we're restoring, reimagining, and translating as part of the **Modern Library of Alexandria** — a global movement to preserve and share humanity's most important ideas.

What was once lost to fire and time is now rising again — not just as memory, but as living, breathing knowledge, freely accessible to all.

What You Can Do Next:

- **Keep Reading.**

  Discover more legendary works — in beautiful print, audiobook, or digital form — at LibraryofAlexandria.com.

- **Build Your Own Library.**

  Every title is available as a paperback, hardcover, or collectible boxset — at true printing cost. Craft a personal library worthy of display.

- **Spread the Light.**

  Share this book. Tell others about the movement. Help us translate every timeless work into every language, so no reader is ever left behind.

By finishing this book, you've already taken part in something extraordinary.

Join us at LibraryofAlexandria.com

Together, we're rebuilding the greatest library the world has ever known.

With appreciation,

The Modern Library of Alexandria Team

Visit:
www.libraryofalexandria.com
Or scan the code below: